MAGGIE WILLIAMS RICHMOND

Course Adjustments

novum pro

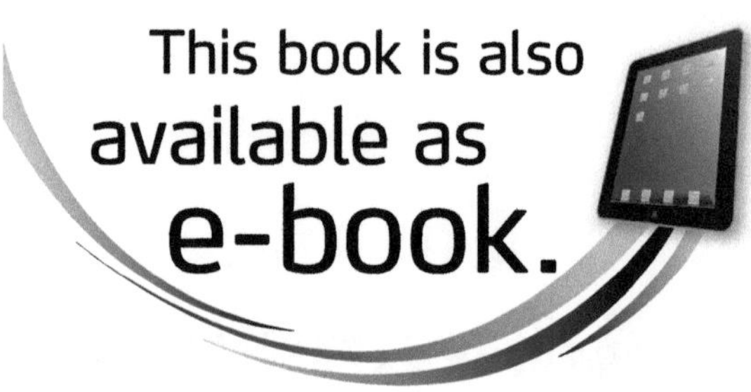

www.novum-publishing.co.uk

© 2022 novum publishing

ISBN 978-3-99131-432-5
Editing: Roderick Pritchard-Smith
Cover photos:
Grafxart, Kriscole | Dreamstime.com
Cover design, layout & typesetting:
novum publishing

www.novum-publishing.co.uk

'PEOPLE WILL NOT LOOK FORWARD
TO POSTERITY WHO NEVER LOOK BACKWARD
TO THEIR ANCESTORS.'

EDMUND BURKE (1729–1797)

**Spring 1625. Seizing
the opportunity for an adventure,
a restless young Scotsman
travels through a foreign war zone
in search of his childhood friend
who has gone missing after
the Battle of Blavet.**

CHAPTER ONE

The dining hall at Hawkhill is exactly as Elspeth likes it to be – a rare occurrence. The fire is burning brightly in the hearth. The shutters are open to let in the spring sunshine and a soft breeze. Her closest family are seated around the long oak table. The dresser is groaningly laden with dishes of fish, pots of vegetables, baskets of baps and bannocks, and the last of the apples and pears, retrieved from the cool scullery where they've been stored since last autumn. Davie and young Harry are topping up the tankards of ale, while Nellie darts to and fro between the hall and the kitchen, where wee Gytha is scouring the pans and longingly eyeing the comfits that are being kept back for the end of this feast.

'Nellie, you've done us proud!' Will says, smiling at the housekeeper.

'Och, Master, thank you – but Gytha's done her fair share, and Master Jack made the breads for us.'

Jack flushes, as all eyes turn to him, and he takes a breath in.

'There's something I'd …' he starts – but he's missed his chance.

'What a shame Billy couldn't join us too,' Elspeth is saying. 'It would've been lovely to have all our nephews together for once, wouldn't it Will?'

Will looks down the table at his sister. 'Aye, it would, but I daresay he can't get away from the inn. Horses don't look after themselves! But it's good that Sandy made it – and kind of the Setons to let him come home.'

Sandy gives a small smug smile and a nod, feeling pleased by his uncle's recognition. It was no trouble to walk the five miles this morning from Pinkie House. He knows he's fallen on his feet, working as a gardener to Lord Winton. He enjoys both the creativity and the labour of the job, and his employer has a rare tolerant attitude, encompassing new ideas as well as old traditions.

Today is a good example. Not everyone was happy when King James re-introduced the celebration of Christmas and Easter. Even fewer people now mark Mothering Sunday, one of the old festival days in Lent, when people used to go back to their 'mother church' where they were baptised. But the Setons, and especially Lord Winton himself, are staunch Catholics. They embrace what others decry as 'Papist nonsense', and today they have given all their staff a rare and welcome day off.

'You must mind and say thank you to his lordship,' Elspeth reminds Sandy, then raises her eyebrows. 'I hope he's not missing these daffs you've brought me?'

'Nae, Auntie,' Sandy replies, havering between amusement and irritation that his aunt still treats him as if he were nine, not nineteen.

'I grew them on my own patch,' he tells her, 'under the apple trees – but the grounds are full of them, a regular sea of yellow!'

'Speaking of seas …' Jack leaps back into the conversation, 'I've something to tell you all.'

'Oh, Jack, just a moment. Nellie's bringing in the pie!'

Jack deflates like a pricked balloon, feeling the weary sort of resignation that his family increasingly provokes. Everyone's attention has turned to the centrepiece of the meal, the meat pie, releasing its delicious savoury aroma as Will slices and serves it. Sighing, Jack chides himself that it's his own fault. He really should have known better than to try to compete for attention with food – and with his three younger brothers. This is how it's been ever since they all came to live here with Aunt Elspeth and Uncle Will, after their foster-grannie, Ma Mayne, died. Lucky for Billy that he inherited her cottage, and for Sandy, that he got to move away for his work. Not that Jack's not glad of this comfortable home, the slightly fussy love of his old-fashioned aunt, the gentle guidance of his uncle – he's just grown out of it. He's twenty-one now. For the last five years, he's been striding day and night to and fro to Leith and back to his work at MacMorran's Mill. It's good work, fetching the grains from the merchant ships at the dock, overseeing the lads to make sure they adjust the grindstone for the oats, the barley, or the wheat … and of course the baking itself. It's served Jack well, and no doubt it will again, but first …

'Could you all please listen a moment? I've some news.'

The babble of voices continues around him, as his family pile their plates high, stretching out for just another spoonful. The youngsters are chewing and talking at the same time, and Sandy is describing his latest planting scheme for the new herb garden at Seton House.

'Please, could you listen?'

At the far end of the table, Will catches the urgency in Jack's tone. He glances across at him and realises that this usually placid and quiet lad is about to erupt.

'Quiet all of you!' he says, not loudly, but in his school-masterly tone that cannot be ignored. A hush falls. Jack blushes and gulps.

'Jack, you've something to tell us,' Will says, looking his nephew in the eye, giving him a smile and an encouraging nod. 'We're listening now. What is it we need to know, eh, lad?'

'Um, it's just, I thought you all should know …'

'You've got a girl!'

'You've lost your job!'

'Harry, Davie, stop sniggering and be quiet. Jack, you're not ill are you?' Elspeth asks, noticing how pale he is.

'No, I'm not ill, and it's not about a girl …' he falters, the interruptions having almost robbed him of his momentum. He takes a deep breath.

'Um, yes, so it is about my job. Well, sort of. I've spoken with Miller MacMorran …'

'Oh,' Elspeth interrupts, 'such a pleasant man. And so good of him to give you your job. But then, his pa always had a soft spot for your dear ma, and you've certainly inherited her talent for baking. I always say …'

'Elspeth, stop,' Will intervenes, laughing. 'You don't know yet what Jack's trying to tell us! Go on lad, make it quick!'

All right then, Jack thinks, *I can do quick!*

'I'm leaving. I'm leaving tomorrow on a ship called Eagle. Miller MacMorran says if I'm home in three months I can have my job back, and until then wee Brodie can take my place ... And if Davie wants it,' he looks at his brother, 'you can take Brodie's place with the other millers.'

'Yes!' Davie punches the air in delight. 'No more school!'

'Um, so that's it really,' says Jack, bowing his head slightly, and peering up from under his brows to gauge his family's reactions. Davie's is obvious, as he begins to lord it over Harry, the youngest of the brood and doomed to another year at school. Sandy gives him a thumbs up – and keeps on eating. Elspeth and Will look thunderstruck. Will recovers first.

'Let me get this straight, Jack. You're leaving the mill for three months, someone called Brodie is taking your place ... and Davie can take Brodie's place ...'

Jack nods. 'Aye, that's it.'

'... and you're going off on a ship called Eagle? God's teeth, lad – sorry, Elspeth – but why? Where's all this coming from? What's happening?'

Will gets up, yanks Harry off his chair next to Jack, and takes his place.

'Harry, go sit in my chair by Davie and Sandy – and mind you all keep the noise down. Your aunt and I need to talk to Jack.'

Pulling faces at his brother, Harry does as he's told, and the three youngsters are happy to get on with their meal – with a few extras since no one is looking. Nellie, popping her head around the door to see that everyone's happy with their meal, sees the serious faces of her master and mistress, and retreats to the kitchen.

I'll hear about it soon enough, she thinks to herself, and turns to the young kitchen maid.

'Gytha, I don't think we'll be needed in the hall for a while, and you've finished the cook-pots, haven't you?'

'Yes, Miss Nellie. They're all done.' Gytha points anxiously at the gleaming stack.

'Then it's time for our dinner. Pass us your plate ...'

Gytha is swift to obey. She's still adjusting to the comforts of life at Hawkhill, after spending all of her twelve years in the poor house. *Surely,* she thinks, *life can't get better than this!*

In the dining hall, Jack is feeling both relieved and sheepish.

'Uncle Will, Aunt Elspeth, I'm sorry to have dropped this on you so suddenly. I didn't know how else to do it. I wanted everyone to know at the same time ...'

'It's all right, Jack,' Will reassures him. 'I know it's hard for you to get a word in edgewise, and you're right to tell us all ...'

'But it's a shock,' Elspeth adds. 'Jack, what's going on? Have you been so unhappy? Could you not have tell't me? Or Uncle Will?'

'Oh, no, please don't think that.' Jack takes his aunt's hand, gives it a gentle squeeze. 'It's not that I've been unhappy, just, ach I don't know, restless? My mates who work on the ships, they're always telling me where they've been, what they've seen – so many strange places, strange people. I suppose I've been envying them, imagining what it must all be like ...'

'And getting itchy feet?' Will suggests.

'Exactly. I can't put my finger on it, but I've felt more and more unsettled for ... oh, for ages now. So when I heard that they're a man down on the Eagle, after Buchan broke his leg and was laid off, I had a word with Master Flint. I'd already met him, of course, had a few drinks with him and the lads whenever they were in Leith. And he's said he'll take me on!'

Telling his tale, Jack is getting his confidence back, feeling that the worst – making his announcement – is over.

'It's great, isn't it? Even 'though I've no experience, never set foot outside Scotland, Flinty – I mean, Master Flint – he says I can go. It'll be hard work, and I've a lot to learn ... but I really need this.' He looks his uncle in the eye. 'I want to do something different, just for a while ...I'm sorry ...'

His voice trails off. Jack's not used to expressing how he feels. It's embarrassing, childish, weak? His head droops again. But suddenly he feels his uncle's strong arms go around him, and he's being hugged so hard he can barely breathe.

'Jack, you're a good lad. I should've told you more often,' Will says, 'and I should've seen that you need a break, aye, and a bit of adventure, mebbe? I can't say it's not a surprise, and I can't say I don't have a few misgivings ... but I know better than to try and stop you. Why, you're older than I was when me and your father, God rest his soul, and our brother Andrew all ran off and joined the army of the Netherlands. Changed all our lives, that did.'

Will's mind flashes back to those days, fighting with the Dutch for their independence from Spain. In amongst the blood and the muck, the fear, the camaraderie, and the occasional bouts of boredom, Will had fallen in love, for the first and only time. Not a day passes but he doesn't remember Pieter; not a night passes but he sees again Pieter's body lying on the battlefield, perfect but for the one deep wound.

All this time, Elspeth has been sitting quietly, picking at her dinner. But now she's had enough.

'And is that all you've got to say to your nephew, Will Balfour? You did it, so he can do it? Mercy on us, I never heard the like! Oh yes,' she carries on, her voice rising as Will begins to protest, 'yes, I'm sure all the three of you thought you were off on a fine adventure. But Hendrie nearly died, that time you brought him home, and then there were all those shenanigans that we won't talk about here ...' She gives Will a stern look, knowing that he knows what she's referring to. 'And Andrew never came home again, just off and marrying the Dutch girl, and then there's you!'

Oh God, Will thinks, conscious of the silence that's fallen around the table, and the four pairs of sharp young ears. *Now what's she going to say!*

'You left the army and just drifted around for years! Och, I know you finally settled down here with me, took up your school-mastering ... And I know you've been a good uncle to these lads here. But honestly Will, I just think if you and Andrew and the boys' father had never gone off to that damn army, it would've been better all round. And now ...'

Elspeth's got the bit between her teeth. Usually so calm and quiet, her fears for her family, for the boys, for Jack especially, sound like anger.

'... yes, now Jack's about to do the same thing, to throw everything up! For the sake of what? An adventure! Ha!'

She looks her nephew up and down.

'Jack, I can't forbid you to go and I won't even try. But I think you're making a very big mistake. So you think, and think hard! Regrets are something it's impossible to get rid of. Now, if you'll excuse me, I'll go for my rest.'

Will and Jack jump to their feet to help her, but she shakes them off. Reaching for her two trusty sticks to lean on, her crooked back making her walk unevenly, her aching legs making her slow, she inches her way to the door and out of the room. No one says a word.

'Nellie!' they hear Elspeth call. 'Help me to my room, if you please.'

As the sound of footsteps diminishes up the stairs, Will and the boys begin to breathe again.

'God's teeth,' Will says, 'I'm sorry about that, lads. You do know it was more directed at me and my brothers than at you all? I never knew my sister was so upset – has been so upset for all these years.'

'But she's not wrong, is she?' Sandy says. 'I mean, about what the army did to you all?'

'Ach, lad, the army was both good and bad, just like anything else. And no one can ever know what would, what might, have happened if we hadn't joined up! But ...'

Will is interrupted by Harry, the youngest. 'I don't want Jack to go. Not unless I can go too! It's not fair. I'll be the only one left, the only one still going to school. I'm fourteen now. I've learned enough!'

'No. You're not leaving school yet. One more year, that's what we agreed, Harry, and then the world's your oyster.' Will turns to Jack. 'Jack, I'm sorry your aunt's upset. But you know, it's out of love, fear and love, for you, for all of you. She just wants to keep you all safe. This is her world and it's small. You know she's never been able to get about much herself. This is all she knows.'

'I still think she's right,' Sandy insists. 'Jack's throwing over a good job, and for what? For a whim!'

'But it means I get to leave school, go and work at the mill,' Davie chips in. 'I think you should go, Jack!'

Will, Jack, and even Sandy, laugh at Davie's self-interested opinion, and the atmosphere relaxes a little.

Jack, who hasn't said a word since his aunt began her harangue, finally speaks.

'I'm sorry I've upset Aunt Elspeth. I'm sorry to have spoilt this meal. I should've told you sooner. But I'm not changing my mind. I'm still going in the morning.'

CHAPTER TWO

The next day dawns grey, with a mist in the air that clings to the skinny branches of the rowan trees, glistens from the intricate spider's webs, and drips onto the cobbled lanes of Restalrig. Jack never gives it a thought. What does the weather matter? After a restless night, he's eager to be off, his pack already stuffed with a few essentials – a change of clothes, a knife, a spoon, a pair of spring scissors, his flageolet, and a small bag of coins. His bedroll is tied on underneath the pack with some stout cord. After a scant wash, he pulls on his tunic, jacket, and breeches, and, carrying his shoes and his pack, creeps down the stairs. There was enough bother yesterday without running into anyone today and starting it all off again, just minutes from leaving. Jack's stomach is already churning with a mixture of excitement and anxiety. But perhaps there's time to filch a couple of the bannocks he made himself and some cheese from the kitchen? If he can't eat them now, he's sure to want something later.

'Jack, there you are lad!'

'Who ...? Oh, Uncle Will! I didn't expect anyone else to be up. I was just ...'

'You were just about to sneak off, weren't you?' Will says with a smile, to show he's not cross. 'I know. Yesterday was enough, wasn't it! But I couldn't let you go off on your own, lad, and besides, you need something in your stomach. Oh yes,' he insists over Jack's protests, 'I know you'll be feeling queasy, but you hardly ate anything yesterday. Look, there's a sausage bap here with your name on it, and this'll wash it down well.'

Will hands Jack a tankard of small beer, takes a deep draught of his own, and they both munch in silence for a few minutes.

'Thanks, Uncle Will. You were right. I don't feel so shaky now!' Jack admits. 'But I'd better get going.'

He hefts his pack onto his back, squinting over his shoulder as his uncle shoves something into the top.

'Just something to see you on,' Will says. 'And I'll walk with you, if I may? I've plenty of time to see you to Leith and get back before old Dunlop rings the school bell.'

Striding away along the lane, the two men are so deep in conversation that they don't hear the call from behind them – 'Jack, wait! Jack? Come back! Please come back. I haven't said goodbye …' – and nor do they turn to see the bent and forlorn figure of Elspeth, propped on one of her sticks at the doorway, her hand waving farewell, her cheeks wet with tears, her heart heavy with regret.

'So the Eagle, she's one of the Baltic traders isn't she?' Will asks.

'Aye,' Jack replies, sounding surprisingly glum. 'I'd hoped to be seeing Riga and Visby and Stettin – don't you just love those names! But no, that's not to be. Flinty says there's too much trouble at the moment, you know, with the Swedes and the Dutch, to make that passage safe. We're bound for Bordeaux and Bilbao, by way of Bruges and La Rochelle.'

'Are you, by God!' Will sounds surprised. 'There's been a fair bit of trouble among the French down that way – but it must be quieter now, or else Master Flint wouldn't take that route.' Will pauses, thinks for a moment. 'Jack,' he asks, 'd'you remember Rab Logan? He used to live at Pitcullo, near your Aunt Missy in Fife.'

'Of course,' Jack replies, smiling. 'We used to mess about with his lads when we visited Missy and Walter – and their lads too. Quite a gang we all were, nine of us – us five, Robin and Jon, and Jamie and Mel.'

'Aye, a load of ruffians! But the thing is, the Logans have moved, did you know? Jesette's father died, so she and Rab are running her family's estate. Her mother's getting on a bit now, and moved in with her sister I believe. There was no one else.

Our second cousin, another William, and his wife Helena Napier, they're at Pitcullo now. Ach, but that's beside the point! What I wanted to say was, if you get the chance, you could p'rhaps visit Rab? I believe it's inland from La Rochelle where they are, near Surgères. The Cosse estate.'

Jack doesn't answer. Visiting old family friends isn't high on his agenda. They walk a few moments in silence, until, glancing at his uncle, Jack notices his faraway and rather sad expression.

'Are you all right, Uncle Will?'

'Och aye.' Will comes out of his reverie. 'I was just remembering what Elspeth spoke about yesterday, how I set off with your pa and your uncle Andrew – off to join the army of the Netherlands. I'd almost forgotten that feeling, that mixture of longing and dread!' Will laughs.

'Exactly!' Jack is both relieved and slightly amazed that a middle-aged schoolmaster might know what it feels like to be off on an adventure.

'Aye, and years later, after I'd come back from Flanders, I met another lad, young Conn – a bit of an Irish rebel he was! It was around the time young Harry was born, and we lost your ma.'

Will pauses, this time remembering Geillis, plump and motherly, always fussing about something, always simple and straight-forward, always loving. He sees in his mind's eye her tangle of mousy-brown curls, her plain and practical clothes, her smooth skin too often pleated in frowns, her warm smile; hears once again her gurgling laugh.

Ach, so sad, to lose such a one. What a fool my brother Hendrie was … and he's gone as well.

Will sighs, realises Jack is watching him with concern, and picks up his story.

'So, anyway, this Conn, he stayed at Missy's house in Fife for a while, fell in love with Sara, the Spanish lassie who was learning from Missy all about the natural remedies and so on, you know?' He pauses again and glances at Jack, who nods.

Aye, Jack thinks, everyone knows about Aunt Missy's weird passion for making lotions and potions, balms and salves, teas and tinctures, from flowers and herbs. Even weirder is that they always seemed to work!

'So this Irishman, Conn?' he prompts.

'Och, it's just that he set off on an adventure, like you're doing. Walked out one summer's morning ... and we never saw him again. I wonder where he ended up? Good lad, quiet, musical – a bit like you ... Mind you don't disappear too, all right!'

With the quayside of Leith coming into view, Jack's excitement bubbles inside him. His chin is up, his eyes are bright, he almost fizzes. Will stops before they get too close, understanding the embarrassment relatives can cause. He gives Jack his usual bear-hug.

'Jack, I'll miss you. Your aunt would be saying 'Don't go drinking and getting into fights!'' Will laughs. 'I know better than that, and I won't even say 'be good' – but you be sure and stay safe, all right? And make the most of your adventure! Now be off with you!'

With one last hug, Jack tears himself away from his wise old uncle, swallows down the lump rising in his throat, and turns to face the Eagle. Sam Campbell is standing alongside, evidently looking out for him, waving and calling. With a hasty farewell – 'Bye, Uncle Will – and thanks for everything!' – Jack joins his friend and, for the first time, boards the Eagle.

Like her sister ship the Swan, and bearing an equally impressive figurehead, with curved beak and wings outspread, Eagle is a pear-shaped Dutch-built fluyt, typical of many of the ships leased by British companies. Swan carried colonists to the Americas, but Eagle is simply a merchant vessel, manageable by a small crew. Fitted out with far fewer arms and much less ammunition, she can carry twice the amount of cargo as those which double as warships – and more cargo means more cash. Another benefit is that the fluyt's shallow draft allows the vessel to bring cargo down rivers and in and out of ports which other ships cannot reach. As soon as Jack has stowed his pack in the cramped crew quarters – and grinned delightedly over both the pack of food and the purse of money that Will tucked into the top – Sam loses no time in showing him everything he needs to know for his first day or so. Before they know it, the square-rigged three-master is out in the Firth of Forth, and Scotland diminishes first to a lump, then a line, then a dot on the horizon. Finally, it disappears entirely.

The next few days pass in a blur for Jack. As the newest recruit with absolutely no experience of sailing, it's just as well that he's quick to learn and to adapt – and that he's a good judge of when it's best to ask questions and when to keep his mouth shut. Already friends with Sam, Jack gets to know Sam's friend Daan, a young Dutchman who has just two voyages under his belt. Daan is delighted not to be the least experienced crewman now that Jack has arrived. Together the three of them cope with the ribald humour, the profanities, and the harsh criticisms of some of the other crew members. But within a week, only the cook, inclined even on the best of days to be surly, still resents the newcomer's presence. Jack is known to have been a baker, and for Cookie anything even vaguely resembling competition is intolerable. To enter the galley, even intending to help, is to enter a danger zone. Jack soon realises he must keep his distance, but in any case, he's plenty busy enough elsewhere. By the time Eagle reaches the canals of Bruges, he's found his feet and has adjusted to the rhythms of sailing.

Jack, Sam, and Daan are determined to make the most of their twelve hours shore leave in the quaint town. They admire the ornate houses lining the labyrinth of canals and peer up at the towering pinnacle of the belfry and carillon in the busy market square. Jack fingers some lace at one of the stalls, and the young saleswoman, bobbin in hand, seizes her chance. After a few minutes of conversation – during which neither Jack nor the girl understand a word the other says – he succumbs to her encouraging smiles and buys a length for Aunt Elspeth, stuffing it into his pocket. It's not too long before, finding themselves outside one of the many inns, the trio sample the local cloudy wheat beer, and the strong malty ale made in the nearby Trappist abbey.

'Mijn vader says Bruges was much more busy in de oude tijd, the old days,' Daan tells them. 'He was a zeeman, like me, but sailing uit Antwerp. He is saying that the Zwin channel here, it is filling with slib – the silt? – and soon it will not be possible. Antwerp is being more important now for the trade.'

'But not as bonny?' Sam suggests.

'Ah, perhaps,' Daan concedes. 'You know the story behind the name Antwerp? No? It comes from a giant who lived by the river Schedlt and cut off the hands of the people who would not pay to go across. In the end, Brabo the hero, he killed the giant and threw his hand into the river.'

Seeing his companions' puzzlement, he adds, 'It is meaning 'to throw', in my language 'hand werpen' – Antwerp!'

Sam and Jack's mocking laughter at this tall tale rings around the square, as Daan protests 'But yes! I am not making it up you know!'

At their next port of call, Southampton, no one is allowed ashore, other than to off-load and re-load cargo. Master Flint is anxious to get across the Narrow Sea, so, to Jack's regret, Eagle does not linger. He would have liked to look around. It was from this port, five years ago, that the Brownists left on the Speedwell and the Mayflower, bound for the New World. The pioneering Puritans come back into Jack's mind some days later, as he enjoys a rare moment of solitude while Eagle passes between Quiberon and Belle-Île-en-Mer. They've been within sight of what Jack thinks of as 'the real Atlantic' for some time now.

To cross it, now that would be a huge adventure, Jack thinks to himself. *Ach, but this isn't bad! The crew are all right, on the whole. A bit of space would be good, a bit of privacy, and not so many mice and lice! With all the snoring and the belching and the farting and the vomiting – although to be fair, the vomiting is mostly myself –*

well, it's just like bunking in with my brothers! And they're all as glad as I am that I've stopped throwing up – well, at least it's not every day now! Coming round by Ushant, oof, that was a bit rough with all those spring storms. It wasn't just me leaning over the side! No, we were all a bit green for a couple of days … But I do believe I'm getting even fitter than I did working the grindstones at the mill and kneading mountains of dough. Och, I wish I'd done this years ago! Why …

A sudden lurch jolts Jack from his musings.

What on earth was that? Ugh!

The hull itself seems to be screeching, and a terrible scraping sound sets his teeth on edge. The deck tips and boxes and crates begin to slide loose of their restraints. Screeeech. The sound comes again, then an enormous thump, and Eagle judders, shudders, flinging cargo and men first forwards and then back.

'All hands!' Master Flint is calling. 'Stir yerselves, ye loungers! Jack, Daan, get those boat hooks and stave us off! You three, down into the bilges and prepare to bale!'

As more of the crew join them in their effort, pushing with all their might against the mass barely visible just under the surface, Eagle gradually floats free. Master Flint is still shouting orders, the crew running hither and thither, digging out hammers, melting a pot of tar, the smothering stink almost overpowering in the cramped space. While some are below, baling as fast as they can, others are making running repairs, bracing a beam across the hull, hammering the struts into place to cover the hole, caulking the whole scruffy mend with smelly black pitch. They work frantically for what feels like forever, fearing the worst, that the repair won't hold and they'll be driven, sinking, onto the rugged Brittany shore.

CHAPTER THREE

It's not good, but it could be worse.

This makeshift repair seems to be holding. Eagle won't sink, but she won't get to Bordeaux – let alone to Bilbao – and home again like this, Master Flint finally decides, cursing himself for not somehow spotting the underwater hazard. Now Eagle has so unceremoniously barged into it, debris can be seen floating lazily away on the waves through a tangled mess of old rigging. A broken mast pokes above the surface.

Damn it to hell! Why did I nae spot that wreck! Ach, but what's done is done. We'll need to shift some of the cargo, but with a fair wind, we should make it.

'There's nowhere here we can stop,' he tells the crew, 'just wee fishing villages, no real harbours, and no shipwrights. We'll have to put in for full repairs at La Rochelle. Ach, and we were making such good time!' He spits with disgust, then turns back to the men. 'If ye're inclined to pray, pray for calm weather and a steady wind. The last thing we need is a gusty storm to tilt us over! Thank God those storms hit before we got here! Aye, but Donald, make sure the gun ports are closed, and then get the cargo shifted across.'

'What was it we hit?' Jack ventures to ask.

'A wreck, by the look of it, lad. Ye ken there was a battle in these waters, a few weeks back? The Huguenot rebels took on the French fleet – and won, by God! I reckon we got caught up with one of the casualties they didn't capture. Ach, at least now yon Frenchie king's retreated, so we shouldnae be troubled … And from what I've heard, Soubise has taken over the islands by La Rochelle.'

'Soubise, Captain?'

'Leader of the rebels. Calls himself 'Admiral of the Protestant Church', whatever that's meant to mean! He controls the waters now from Nantes to Bordeaux – and them's the waters we're in! Wherever we dock, we'll be in his debt. It'll likely take a while to get Eagle fixed, so mind yer manners, all of ye! We're not looking for trouble. D'ye hear me, Gus? Douggie? Now, back to work, the lot of ye!'

The next day, Eagle limps her way through a light sea-mist and into the harbour of La Rochelle. Master and crew are all relieved, but the news is not good: it may take up to a week to make proper repairs – a week they can ill-afford – but Master Flint has no choice. He calls the crew together again.

'Right lads, this is how it is. There's nothing for it but to get this fixed good and proper, else we'll be going nowhere! We'll need to take off most of the goods and store them. If we all give a hand with that, and then Frank, Douggie, Gus, Sam, and Daan, ye'll all stay here with me and help with the repair. It'll get done quicker and cheaper – and in any case, I'd like to see what yon Frenchies do to her.'

He slaps the bow rail proprietorially with a gnarled brown hand, narrowing his eyes as he surveys the rest of his crew.

'The rest o' ye, the quicker she's emptied, the sooner ye can be off into the town. If ye come back here early, ye'll be put to work! But like I said before, no trouble, else ye'll be answering to me, never mind yon Soubise and his men! I'll send word when we're ready to leave. Well, get on with ye, get started!'

The crew work hard to empty Eagle, forming a line and passing everything along and into a warehouse that Master Flint has commandeered for the duration. They work all day and it's still not quite finished. They're all glad to fall into their hammocks and bunks at nightfall. The following day, it only takes an hour to stow the remaining cargo and a cheer goes up among those released once it's done. Jack was at first disappointed to be considered expendable and not kept back with Sam and Daan, but now he realises this is his chance to go and visit the Logans as Uncle Will suggested. To be honest, he hadn't intended to. He'd been told that the stop at La Rochelle was usually as brief as that at Southampton, so fate has played into his hands. With his pack once again on his back, Jack stands on the dock getting his bearings, looking up first at the pointed Lantern Tower that acts as a lighthouse and then at the chain towers of Saint Nicolas and La Chaîne, one square, one round.

Good job there was no chain between them yesterday, he thinks, *to keep poor old Eagle out! But enough standing and gazing – I've twenty-odd miles to walk to Surgères!*

Rocking slightly as he once again becomes accustomed to a surface that doesn't lurch in all directions, Jack heads east.

The walk from La Rochelle to Surgères is an easy one, along a tree-lined lane over the flat land, just a few isolated hamlets and farmsteads basking under the huge sunlit sky. He doesn't know it, but Jack is walking along an old Roman road, known as Le Grand Chemin. The Romans had been in control of Celtic Gaul for some five centuries, until they were overpowered by the Franks, over a thousand years ago. One of their legacies was a network of highways, radiating from their capital and reaching out to the fringes of their empire. Jack is simply glad of this long straight track. It passes through an area once covered by the ancient forest of Argenson, but now vines and sunflowers have replaced the trees. They seem strange and exotic to a young Scotsman, more accustomed to heather moorlands and peaty bogs. Jack makes one just detour, having sighted a small town a little way off to the left.

It must be dinner time by now, and surely there'll be an inn?

He's not disappointed. The auberge at Aigrefeuille-d'Aunis provides him with a hearty meal and a flagon of the excellent local white wine. Much restored, and with a feeling of great goodwill towards the world at large, Jack meanders back to the road, arriving in Surgères as the sun begins to sink and people are beginning to emerge for their evening promenade.

'Excuse me … um, excusez-moi, monsieur. Où est la maison du domaine Cosse? Um, Monsieur Logan et Jesette Cosse? Connaissez-vous leur maison?'

'La maison Cosse? Oui, bien sûr. Tout le monde connaît la maison de l'ambassadeur, Dieu repose son âme. C'est là-bas, la rue Traversière, la maison blanche.'

'Merci, monsieur. Bonsoir.'

'Je vous en prie … Mais monsieur, il n'y a personne là-bas. C'est vide. Ils sont partis.'

'Merci encore! Bonsoir.'

Jack had forgotten that Jesette's late father had been an ambassador to the court of King James at Holyrood and Westminster, but it explains why the man knew the house.

I didn't understand any of the last sentences, but no matter, he thinks. *Why, this is easy! My first time alone on foreign soil, and I've had a drink and a meal, arrived in the town I wanted, and asked for and been given directions. Rue Traversière, a white house. Nothing to it!*

Jack is pleased with himself. Striding off, absorbed in his self-congratulations, he entirely forgets that, according to his Uncle Will, the Cosse estate is outside the town, not on one of the main streets in the centre. He knocks on the grey painted door of the elegant white townhouse. No answer. He knocks again, nothing. Finally, he notices that the shutters are all closed. There are no signs of life at all.

Damn! Is that what the man was saying? They must have gone out. Now what to do?

He looks around as if the answer will materialise out of thin air. Across the small square, an old woman, basket in hand, is going into her house.

'Ah, excusez-moi, madame?'

She turns, looks him up and down, sweaty from his day's hike, face flushed from wine and sunshine, a rip in his breeches.

'Oui? Qu'est-ce que tu veux?'

'Um, cette maison, c'est la maison Cosse? Rab Logan? Jesette?'

'Oui c'est la maison de l'ambassadeur Cosse, mais la famille n'est pas ici. Ils sont au domaine.'

Taking pity on Jack's total puzzlement, the neighbour offers her best English.

'Gone! Monsieur Logan et Jesette, gone to la ferme, the farm.'
Merde! This is not good news.

Almost drowning in a flood of French, both hampered and assisted by various passers-by, Jack learns that the family are at the Cosse estate near Marans. *Of course,* Jack remembers too late. *Uncle Will did say outside Surgères.* And there's something else he's being told –

Am I understanding any of this? I think they're saying that Rab is unable to make a voyage because of something to do with a horse. What? And Marans is twenty miles away?

'But I've just walked twenty miles from La Rochelle!'

Ah yes. The general consensus is that it would have been better not to come to Surgères.

Well, thanks! I agree with that, thinks Jack, *but I'm here now, for better or worse!*

'Il y a un auberge ici? Pour la nuit pour moi?'

Of course there is an inn. There are several inns, and Jack's new friends are happy to discuss their relative merits and de-merits for a long time. Just as he's about to sit down on the cob-bles and lay his head on his pack, Jack feels someone's bony hand take his arm in a firm grip –

Uh-oh, now what?

– but the accompanying words prove more reassuring than threatening.

'Monsieur, I show you inn. Good inn. Food, bed, oui?'
Definitely oui.

With much handshaking and many mercis Jack is extract-ed and taken to what indeed proves to be a good inn, with good wine, great cheese, *and not bad bread at all,* thinks the former bak-er. The bent old man who rescued him is happy to be rewarded with his supper, and with a bizarre conversation which neither of them quite understand. Eventually, his new friend excuses himself – 'Je dois rentrer chez ma femme!' – and Jack staggers up the stairs to his narrow bed.

With the slightly sore head, thick tongue, and dry mouth of those unaccustomed to wine, Jack is back on the road early the next day.

'Saint Jean du Liversay, then head for Marans. The Cosse estate is on the left. If I get to the village, I've gone too far. I'll hear it before I see it.'

Like a series of mantras, Jack repeats to himself the instructions he thinks he was given last night when his rescuer and the patron took great pains in discussing his route.

What does that mean, I'll 'hear it before I see it?' It doesn't make sense; he puzzles as he walks. *Perhaps I've misunderstood?*

But soon he's into his stride and reviving in the fresh air, the track he's on again straight and level.

If I didn't know this was a different route, I'd think I was repeating yesterday all over again ... but today, I just hope I find Rab, otherwise it's back to La Rochelle for me, and be put to work!

Jack's wish is granted. Just as the rooftops of the village of Marans appear on the horizon, a cacophony of sound stops him in his tracks.

Is this what they meant, I'd hear it first?

The 'it' is the noise of innumerable chickens, a field full of them, scritching and scratching under the trees, filling the air with harsh squawks, shrill cackles, and triumphant crowing. This must be it – and a roadside sign stating 'Cosse' confirms it. Jack turns left and heads along the rutted track towards an old stone farmhouse. He stops short as a large dog comes barking and bounding towards him.

'Tou-tou, non! Bad dog!'

A lanky boy hurtles out of the house, grabs the dog's collar just in time to stop it from hurling itself at Jack.

'Pardon, monsieur. Il n'est pas méchant. Il aime dire bonjour aux inconnus!'

'Ach, nae worries, lad. I mean, um, pas problème ...'

'Oh, you're Scottish!'

The boy releases the dog and gives Jack a long look through his piercing blue eyes. The dog contents himself with sniffing and slobbering on Jack's boots, and much wagging of his plumy tail.

'It's been a while but … are you … um … you're not Jack are you? Jack Balfour?'

'Yes! And you're Jon. Of course! By God, you've grown!'

The two young men are delighted, slapping each other's backs and grinning.

'Jack! Whatever are you doing here? Where've you come from?'

'I've come from La Rochelle, off my ship, by way of Surgères.'

'Good Go … I mean, goodness! That was a long way round! And off a ship? I thought you were a baker at one of those mills in Leith. Come in and tell us all what's to do. Ma and Pa will be amazed to see you. Did you know Pa's laid up?'

Chattering excitedly, Jon leads Jack into the house. In the salon, Rab is half-sitting, half-lying on the settle, one bandaged leg up, more bandages visible around his chest under a loose tunic, and his left hand in some sort of splint.

'God bless my soul, Jack Balfour! How marvellous! But what on earth are you doing here?'

'He's come off his ship, Pa, from La Rochelle, by way of Surgères!' Jon repeats to his father, as Jesette bustles into the room, wiping her floury hands on a cloth. She's followed by a young woman – a rather pretty young woman with long curly hair – whom Jack takes to be a maid of some sort since she fetches a pot of tea and then disappears again.

There's a lot to catch up on. Jack brings them up to date on how the rest of the family are. Yes, Aunt Elspeth is her usual sweet and crotchety self, Billy's engaged, Sandy's creating a herb garden for Lord Seton … Finally he tells his own news. He's pleased with his tale, of how he had the chance to join Eagle, how they've had to put in for repairs after being holed by a submerged wreck, how Uncle Will particularly said he should visit. In return, Jack learns that Rab fell off his horse – 'Bloody fool thing to do!' Rab says – and now has a broken hand, a broken leg, cracked ribs, and very bruised pride. He's not able to get about, otherwise they'd all be in town, in Surgères, leaving the estate manager, Morel, to look after things here.

'And you're raising chickens?' Jack asks. 'I saw a field full of them … and I was told I'd hear the estate before I see it!'

Rab laughs. 'Yes, we've got a lot of chickens! They're naturally woodland birds, so we let them roam free. Not having them cooped up in sheds stops them from being smelly too! Some are for eggs and some for meat. But we have a vineyard as well, and a few crops. There's a new plant I want to try, brought back from the Americas,' Rab says. 'Indian corn, they call it. Said to be good fodder for cattle. I've recently introduced a small herd of Charolais, so I'll see how they get on with it.'

'And you, Jon, what are you up to?'

'Oh, I usually stay here, to look after the farm,' the lad says, '… Um, with Monsieur Morel of course,' he adds more modestly, after a wry look from his mother.

'Oui,' Jesette confirms with a smile, 'Jon is becoming a very good farmer. It's in his blood from my grand-père.'

'And Robin? Where is he now?'

Silence falls as Jack asks this innocent question, and the atmosphere immediately feels strained. Jesette's face falls and goes pale.

'We don't know,' she says, her blue eyes wide now, and anxious. 'We haven't seen him or heard from him for more than a month.'

CHAPTER FOUR

As Jesette speaks, the pretty young woman comes back into the salon and makes as if to remove the tea things.

'Oh, Jeanne, don't worry about that now. Come, you must meet Jack Balfour, an old friend from Scotland. Jack, this is Jeanne Rouane, Robin's fiancée.'

Robin's fiancée?

Jack gets to his feet, offers a bow, racks his brain for the right thing to say, glad once again that they learnt French at school. The use of the language had both its supporters and its detractors, having been in common usage at the old court and among the ruling classes before King James acceded to the throne of England just over twenty years ago. A lot has changed since then.

'Enchantée, mademoiselle.'

Jeanne gives him a shy bob, her hair falling over her face. 'Monsieur Jacques.'

'Jeanne, we were just about to tell Jack about Robin,' Jesette says.

'Bien sûr, of course. Per'aps Monsieur Jacques will be knowing something we are not.'

'Goodness, I doubt it!' Jack says, feeling unaccountably embarrassed by Jeanne's suggestion. 'But please, do tell me what's happened.'

Between them, Rab, Jesette, Jon, and Jeanne tell Jack that Robin – '… You know how he loves anything to do with the sea?' – had joined the Huguenot naval forces back in January.

'Aye. I've heard about all the Huguenots,' Jack says. 'Benjamin de Rohan, is that right, duc de Soubise? He commands the Huguenot rebels here on the west coast and at sea?'

Jack is pleased that he knows a little about this. He and the rest of the crew had talked about it all since Eagle was holed. Knowing nothing about the conflict before now, Jack had learnt that the Huguenots were similar in some ways to the Puritans of Britain but, some said, more political than they were religious. They'd first rebelled in southern France about five years ago when their lands were annexed by the king's forces, and an exclusively Catholic parliament was created. The Huguenot leaders, the two Rohan brothers, were staunch Protestants who had taken part in the Dutch war of independence, and they aimed to create their own state, modelled on the Dutch Republic. However, the Huguenots were less successful against the French than the Dutch had been against the Spanish. The rebellion failed. Recently their resentment had once again increased, as King Louis blatantly ignored the terms of the treaty between them.

'So in January, Soubise made a surprise attack on the French fleet, captured it, and now controls this whole area,' Rab tells Jack. 'He's the new master of La Rochelle, and his troops, both soldiers and sailors, are occupying the two islands, the Île de Ré and the Île d'Oléron. You must have seen his fleet when you sailed in?'

'Aye, we did. A great crowd of ships, sixty or seventy I'd say. We were all talking about it on Eagle. It's a pretty impressive sight! But tell me, what's happened to Robin?'

'Ach, Jack lad, we don't know. So keen he was, we didn't have the heart to stop him joining Soubise, doing his bit for the Protestant cause. Well, to be honest with you, he was more interested in doing his bit for a minority, who were being treated unfairly and persecuted. I'm not sure that religious affiliation came into it much.'

Rab glances at his wife and son, then goes on, 'We're a Protestant family, but we've tried to bring up both our boys to value virtues such as justice and fairness, aye, and to think for themselves rather than to blindly follow dogma. I saw enough trouble between Catholics and Reformers when I was a lad. Your own grandfather, Jack, Lord Pittendreich, he was caught up right in the middle of it ... Aye, and your Aunt Missy, she went on quite a quest to find out the truth hidden under a great mountain of lies and rumours. But it was all resolved when she found a document that totally exonerated her father and confirmed the estates as part of the heritage that came to his children. You should ask Missy about it sometime.'

Jesette rolls her eyes and looks askance at Rab as he enthuses about his 'old friend' Missy. She's always wondered exactly what their relationship was, whether there was more to it than her husband will admit. Jack doesn't notice. He is bemused.

Aunt Missy, off on a quest? Surely not! I definitely want to know more about this!

But Rab is returning to the matter in hand.

'Ach, but I'm getting away from the point,' Rab says, 'which is that Robin's certainly got nothing against Catholics personally – has he, Jeanne?'

He laughs as Jeanne blushes, and explains, 'Jeanne's family are Catholic.'

'The thing is,' Jon chips in, 'Robin went off with Soubise and there was this battle, at Blavet, off the Brittany coast?'

Jack nods. 'Yes of course. That's where we ran onto the wreck.'

'How exciting – and scary! When we heard they'd all come back to the islands, we thought Robin would be home soon.' Jon pauses, swallows, takes a deep breath. 'But he's never come back and there's been no word. I said I'd go ...' He stops as his mother gives him a quelling look.

'We've sent messages of course,' she says, her expression sad, her eyes tired, 'but no one seems to know anything.'

Jack speaks before he thinks.

'Well, if he'd been killed, you'd have been told for sure ... Oh, sorry, I don't mean ... but, well, you would, wouldn't you? So in a way, that's good ...' Jack's voice trails off.

Oh God, he thinks, *stop now, I'm making it worse.*

But Rab smiles at him.

'I think you're right, Jack, and I take comfort from it. But it's hard not knowing.'

He looks at his wife and at Jeanne, both, Jack realises, looking pale and strained now their welcoming smiles have been allowed to fade.

'If it weren't for my damn leg and these damn ribs, I'd go to the islands myself, find out what's what.'

'But you cannot,' Jesette confirms. 'You must rest, rest and heal. And no, Jon, I know you keep asking, and I know you would go, but I can't let you. I've lost one son ...'

As Jesette falters, wiping tears from her eyes and then clutching Jeanne's hand tightly, Jack finds himself once again speaking before he thinks.

'I'll go. I'll go and find out from someone on these islands. Eagle's stuck in La Rochelle anyway. I'll go for you and find out what's happened to Robin.'

Even as Jack hears his own words, even as a voice in his head asks what has he done now, the room erupts in a babble of excitement, concern, and, most of all, thanks.

'Oh Jack, really? You'd do that for us? Oh, thank you!'

'Jack, are you sure? Bless you, lad. It's been driving me mad, that I can't go myself. I'd be so grateful ...'

'Jack, that's great! Go and fetch my wretched brother home ...'

'Monsieur Jacques, je vous remercie! Je viendrai, I will come, avec toi ...'

This last comment cuts through the hubbub.

'What? You're saying you'll come with me? No. Non. Mademoiselle Jeanne, you cannot come. It would not be safe. I'll be fine, but ...'

They are all agreed. Jack will go, Jeanne will not.

'Jeanne, it's no place for a girl like you. An army camp! Well, all right then, a navy camp – it makes no difference. Sorry, but you can't go.'

Rab and Jesette are adamant, Jeanne is bitterly disappointed.

'Qu'importe si je suis une fille? Je suis sa fiancée. C'est juste que je lui trouve. It is right for me to find him. Why does it matter I am a girl?' Even in her distress, Jeanne mixes her French and English so that their guest will understand.

'Jeanne, be reasonable,' Rab pleads. 'I know it's hard, but it does matter that you're a girl, fiancée or not. Let Jack go. It'll be a rough enough place for him! He doesn't want to have to worry about you as well – and neither do we.'

Jeanne remains unconvinced. Sitting at home waiting is not for her.

'If I was a boy, you would not be saying this. And if I was a boy, I would have gone days ago!'

Jon scowls, feeling criticised, ashamed that he's thus far obeyed his parents, but Jeanne doesn't notice.

'Ah, it is like for my heroine,' she rattles on, 'my namesake, Jeanne d'Arc. She was my age, and the king himself allowed her to go with the army. She was burned at the stake in my home town of Rouen, and she is a symbol for us, for me! I did not go alone, but I will come with you, Jacques. I can dress like a man, as Jeanne did. No one will know.'

Jeanne's voice is taut, and her passionate outburst silences them all. Jack is the first to speak.

'Jeanne, you are very brave, and Robin is a lucky man. But please, let me go alone. I daresay you're entirely capable of look-ing after yourself, but Rab's right. I'd feel responsible for you – it's just how I've been brought up, you know – and that would be a distraction for me. I know nothing of the situation on the islands, so I need to focus on Robin. And you need to trust me.'

Seeing her face change from flushed back to pale, Jack senses that he has won. Keen to press his point home, he adds, with a glance at Rab.

'I'll go first thing tomorrow and be back the day after that, I promise … if perhaps Rab will lend me a horse I'm not like-ly to fall off!'

His words have done the trick, both persuading Jeanne to let him go alone, and lightening the tense atmosphere. Giving the girl a big hug, Jesette suggests they start making some supper for everyone. Once they've gone into the kitchen, Rab, Jon, and Jack eye one another.

'God's teeth, that was close!' Rab lets out a breath he was hardly aware of holding. 'Well done Jack. I think we're all due a glass of wine after that, don't you!'

The following morning, Jack makes his way slightly warily to the stable block. Jon has said he'll get one of the horses ready for his ride to the Île de Ré, and Jack is hoping it won't be the one that threw Rab.

'Jack, you're looking mighty fearful! Come on in, they won't bite!'

'No, they just throw you off!' Jack hears himself saying, but fortunately, Jon just laughs.

'Ach, that was Pa's own fault. What a man of his age thought he was doing, setting Oak to face a hedge that high, I've no idea!'

'Oak?'

'That's the name of his stallion. We get all our horses from your cousin Mitch's stable in Fermanagh. You know he breeds them for racing? Well, they're not all up to the mark, but they're still mighty fine – and we're mighty glad to have them! Ever since he was a wean, Mitch has named his horses after trees, God only knows why! So we've got Oak and Thorn, Ash and Poplar, and Jeanne's mare, Cherry. But no, I'm not sending you off on Oak. Pa said you don't have horses at home?'

'No. We don't have stables in Restalrig. The last time I rode, ach, it must've been last autumn. I was over in Fife near your old stamping ground, and I went out hunting with Walter.'

'Well, I've got Thorn saddled for you. He's Robin's favourite, good and steady but not dull, you know?'

Jack hasn't got a clue but nods anyway. A few minutes later he's given Thorn a carrot – 'Be kind to me, horse, all right?' – is mounted, and out on the lane.

'Don't go back by way of Surgères,' Jon teases him, holding Tou-tou back from going along with Jack. 'Take the field path over there to Andilly and Villedoux – don't blink or you'll miss them! – then straight on to La Rochelle. You'll need all your charm to get over to the island on the ferry – or a few coins might do the trick, like crossing the Styx!'

'What? Oh, in the Greek myths! Aye, but then I'd be dead, and I'd rather be coming back for another feast like last night! All right then, I'm off. See you tomorrow!'

Jon was right about Thorn. He is good and steady, and Jack's confidence comes back.

It makes a change from walking, he thinks, *'though I'm afraid I'll have stiff legs and a sore backside for the next few days.*

Once again he passes through tiny hamlets set in the wide-open landscape. The sky today is cloudier, and as he gets nearer to the coast the wind picks up. There's a distinct salt tang in the air. Jack snuffs it up gladly. Only twenty-four hours, and he's already missing the sea. Reaching the outskirts of La Rochelle, Jack decides to go and have a sneaky peek at Eagle before trying to cross to the Île de Ré. He guides Thorn towards the harbour, hooves clattering over the old cobblestones. The ship has been hauled out of the water and heeled over on the dockside – and there are Sam and Daan, just about to saunter away. It seems Jack has arrived at just the right time.

'Jack! What the devil are you doing back here,' Sam asks, 'and on such a very fine horse!'

Jack dismounts with a groan, shakes his legs, and pats Thorn's neck.

'Ach, my friend Robin's got caught up with the Huguenots. He hasn't been in touch with his parents, and they're worried. I said I'd go over to the island, find out what's what. This is his horse, Thorn.'

'You're going to the island? To the Huguenots? Good luck with that, mate! We've been hearing about them these last couple of days, and it sounds a bit rough. Will you join us for dinner first? The inn we're staying at – auberge I should say! – has a stable. I'm sure they'll take Thorn in while we eat.'

I could get used to this, Jack thinks, raising a hand in farewell to his friends two hours later. *Very civilised, this long dinner time. Now then Thorn, let's find the ferryman before Master Flint sees us and ropes us in to the repair work!*

It's not far from the dock, but the welcome is far less friendly. The ferry is guarded.

'Arrête là, garçon. Qui es-tu? Que veux-tu?'

The firmly held pike, its point slightly lowered towards Jack, and the expression on the guard's face, make his message plain.

This is no time to forget my French, Jack thinks.

'Pardon, monsieur. Je cherche mon ami. Je pense qu'il est avec le duc, sur l'île. C'est possible … Oh!'

Jack's jaw drops as the guard jumps to attention, holds his pike upright, and sketches a salute.

'Mon Seigneur!'

'What? No, um, if you could just let me on to the ferry … '

A deep laugh from behind him startles Jack so that he nearly topples off Thorn. *What the …*

'Englishman, what do you want with us, eh?'

'Scotsman, thanks all the same!' Jack replies tersely, even before he skews round on Thorn to see who is speaking.

On a white horse is a man dressed in black – like something out of a story, Jack will later say – his hair similarly black and curly, cut short just above the white ruff around his neck. He has a very neatly trimmed beard, and a slightly flamboyant moustache beneath his aquiline nose. His eyes are bright, missing nothing.

'Och aye!' the man laughs, in a terrible accent. 'And what is a Scotsman' he emphasises the word with a slight bow in Jack's direction 'doing in my territory?'

With an alacrity born of panic – and more than a little fear – Jack is off Thorn and proffering his best bow.

'Monsieur le Duc? Pardon. Je ne connais …um, savais … pas …'

Soubise raises his eyebrows at Jack. 'I think, Scotsman, that my English is per'aps a little better than your French? I prefer my language not to be as damaged as my people have been!'

And then he smiles. 'Per'aps you are from this ship that my enemies' hulk has holed, yes?'

'Yes, my lord. I am from Eagle, but now I am seeking out my friend. He is one of your own men. He has been missing since the sea battle, and his family are anxious. He is only young,' Jack explains, then suddenly stops, his mind going round and round.

This is the duke himself! And here am I gabbling on!

'What is the name of this 'only young' man?'

'Robin Logan, my lord.'

'And you? Are you Logan also?'

'No, my lord. I am a friend of the Logan family. I am Jack Balfour from Midlothian … um, near Edinburgh, in Scotland, sire.'

'Balf-our? Jacques Balf-our? But I know this name!' Soubise frowns, casting his mind back. 'Ah oui, bien sûr! Jacques, when I was about your age, I was a soldier in the army of the Netherlands, fighting for the republic against the Spanish overlords. And we won in the end. It was a good apprenticeship for me! Now I am fighting against the French overlords. Always the same story, one faith against another, always the same oppression, the powerful against the less, the many against the few, conform or die. Ha! But I am forgetting … When I was in Flanders, all those years ago, I met three Scotsmen, Balf-our like yourself. A little older than me. Good men, they were, and they fought hard. I don't know what happened to them. They were brothers. Guillaume and Hendrie and … I forget the name of the other. Ah!' Soubise pauses, reading Jack's face, 'I can see these are your people, yes?'

'Yes, my lord, indeed they … they, um, they are my people.' Jack stutters out his reply.

'So tell me,' Soubise says, dismounting, handing the reins to the surprised guard, 'who are they to you, my old comrades, eh? And what became of them?'

'Hendrie was my father, sire, and Guillaume – we call him Will – and Andrew are my uncles. Andrew married a Dutch woman and they settled in Bergen-op-Zoom. My father died, five years after my mother, so after our grandmother died my brothers and I were brought up by Uncle Will. He gave up the army … I think something happened; I don't know what. But anyway, he is a schoolmaster now in Leith.'

'Mon Dieu! Guillaume, Will, un professeur. Incroyable! And I am still fighting … It was très triste, tragique, quand l'amant … Excuse me, I am saying it was tragic when his friend of the heart was killed. So young, so brave. I have never forgotten. And your uncle, ah, he was a broken man.'

For a moment, Soubise is lost in his memories and doesn't notice Jack's astonishment.

Uncle Will's 'friend of the heart'? His lover? And he was killed?

This is all news to Jack. But Soubise is speaking again.

'It was long ago.' He shakes his head, returns to the present. 'So, your friend, the one you seek, what is his name again?'

'Robin Logan, sire, from Surgères. His mother is Jesette Cosse, the ambassador's daughter.'

'Bien sûr! A fine man, Ambassadeur Cosse. And it is his petit fils, his grandson, you seek? Come then! We will cross together and find this rouge-gorge, this Robin!'

CHAPTER FIVE

The Île de Ré lies a mere two miles off the rocky limestone shore of the mainland, on the Atlantic side of a narrow strait known as the Pertuis d'Antioche. Long ago it was an archipelago of three small islands, but over the centuries the increased harvesting of sea salt, combined with natural silting, have linked the three. More recently, fishing locks have been constructed, trapping the fish which come in with the tide, retaining them as it goes out. Once busy not only with fishing but also with trade in salt and wine, both land and water are now given over to the Huguenot occupation. On the short ferry crossing, while their horses are attended to by two of Soubise's men, the duke has a proprietorial air.

'You know of course of our struggle against the French king,' he says to a rather awe-struck Jack. 'We seized this island in janvier. Three hundred soldiers, one hundred sailors – a good enough force. After we returned from the bataille last month, we occupied the Île d'Oléron aussi. It is bigger, and there are more of my men there, but here is better for me, to be near the town, and a better harbour for the ships. Only twelve we had, but now, we have seventy ships, and one is la Vierge, the biggest warship ever built, with eighty cannon. Do you see it there?' Soubise points proudly. 'Oui, la Vierge et aussi le Saint Jean, le Saint Michel, le Saint Charles, le Saint Francois, le Saint Basile …' He laughs. 'All the saints! Ah oui, but aussi la Louise.'

By now the ferry is pulling in to the jetty. Jack is not quite sure what is expected of him, but Soubise soon resolves the matter. A group of men are waiting for their leader's arrival.

'Joubert!' he calls to a tall, thin, pale young man. 'Viens ici! Nous avons un invité, un Écossais. Il est descendu du navire Eagle.' He nods at Jack. 'Il est le fils de mon vieux camarade d'armes. Vous l'aiderez à retrouver son ami, le petit-fils de l'Ambassadeur Cosse.'

Turning back to Jack, Soubise reassures him. 'Joubert will help you to find your friend, the ambassador's grandson. You will be safe with him. I have told him you are the son of my old comrade-at-arms and that you come from the Eagle. He will tell me what he discovers.'

'Merci, mon Siegneur,' Jack replies, bowing and blushing. 'Vous êtes très gentil. C'est un honneur de vous rencontrer'

Clapping him so hard on the back that he almost staggers, Soubise grins. 'Ah, non. You bring me memories of a younger time! Salute your uncle Guillaume for me. He is a good man.'

'I will, surely. Thank you.'

'Joubert,' Soubise again addresses Jack's new companion, 'faites-moi savoir ce qui est arrivé au rouge-gorge, l'ami de notre invite, monsieur Balf-our.'

As Joubert and Jack bow, Soubise strides away, surrounded by his men.

By God, Jack thinks. *That's how to be a leader of men!*

But Joubert is speaking.

'Monsieur Balf-our,' he begins, 'please, you come to the room to be wait, and I will ask for your ami.'

'Please, call me Jack.'

'Jacques, bien. I am name Paul. Et le nom, the name, de votre ami?'

'Robin Logan. He is only young. He came to help at the battle, and we don't know where he is, or what has happened.'

'Je vais le découvrir, Jacques. Be not worry. I will go and discover. He is also Écossais?'

'His father is Écossais, his mother is French, the daughter, la fille, of Ambassador Cosse.'

'Bien. I return tout de suite.'

Paul Joubert is as good as his word. Jack scarcely has time to check on Thorn and take a brief walk around the bay. He is longing to strip off his boots, to feel the sand between his toes and to splash in the water – but perhaps not quite the thing to do right here and right now, Jack decides. His mind is full not of Robin, but of his Uncle Will.

So Uncle Will had a friend, a lover, killed all those years ago? He's certainly never shown any interest in anyone else, Jack realises, *men or women. Ach, poor old Will. I wonder …*

'Monsieur Balf-our, Jacques!'

Jack is startled out of his thoughts and realises he is being summoned. Turning away from the sand and the tempting blue water, he sees Joubert waiting for him, another man, older, by his side.

'Jacques, this is Gaston. He is with your friend Robin in le bataille. He is telling you what is happen.'

Gaston is the opposite of Joubert, short, stocky, and grizzled, his weather-beaten face lined with wrinkles, his tawny hair streaked with grey.

'Monsieur, bonjour. Vous êtes avec mon ami?' Jack is determined to do his best with these Frenchmen.

Gaston shakes Jack's hand with a crushingly firm grip. 'Bonjour Monsieur Jacques. Oui, I am with your friend, the young Rob-in. S'il vous plaît, we sit and I am telling you.'

'Merci. But first, please, he is not hurt, um, bless? Or worse?'

'Non, 'e is not blessé, and il n'est pas mort, dead. When I am see 'im last, 'e is good. I will tell you.'

Perching on the rocks by the soughing sea, Gaston tells his tale. He tells it well, making the most of the drama. It was January. Word had come that the royalist troops were preparing warships off the coast of Normandy, to be used to blockade La Rochelle, already a Huguenot stronghold. Soubise, always a man of action, resolved to outwit the enemy and strike first. They set sail from Chef de Baie, rounding the Île de Ré, twelve boats, full of soldiers and sailors including the young Robin, fired up with enthusiasm for the cause, eager to learn, quick and popular. It was stormy. There seemed to be no division between the grey sea and the grey sky. Towering waves came crashing over the bows, as the wind blew them hither and thither. At last, they cut through the darkness to see the six royal ships at anchor, well-armed with cannon, but very few men visible on board. Out of the storm and the night, Soubise's forces attacked. Boom! went the cannon. Crack! went the firearms. The air was heavy with the smell of gunpowder and full of tiny splintering shards of debris. The king's ships tried to cast off – but there was nowhere for them to go. They were surrounded by the Huguenots, caught in the trap. Finally, two ships managed to break through, and came alongside the smaller Huguenot vessels, each trying to board the other. They were fighting one another in disorder, every man for himself, while all around the blasts continued and the fires began. One of the king's fleet was holed, a gaping maw in its stern. More cannon fire, boom! and it was filled with flame, sinking, sinking, as its crew threw themselves overboard, joined by many others, all abandoning their ships. Suddenly it was all over, the advantage of surprise winning the day for Soubise.

'We are comme les pirates! We come to them furtivement, with stealth? And now we 'ave their ships,' Gaston says with great satisfaction, rubbing his calloused hands together. 'Oui, nous avons tous leur navires, all their ships but the one which we sanked …' He pauses, looks at Jack with a gleam in his eye. 'And your ship found it!' He guffaws. 'Ah, I sorry! Sorry for damage to Eagle, but is funny, non? Et bien, maintenant, now, we are 'ere on les îles and in La Rochelle. Le roi, 'e is lost 'is navy, so now 'e is afraid. Ha!'

'And my friend, Robin Logan?' Jack ventures to ask, blinking himself back to the here-and-now, his imagination having been caught and held in the exciting tale of the sea battle.

'Ah oui. Le petit rouge-gorge, 'e is not sailor, no, 'e is knowing not'ing! But 'e is vite, fast, and 'e is running everywhere, fetching this, getting that, loading les canons, esquiver les dangers … Oui, il est un bon garçon, 'e stay at my side, 'e do as I am say, 'e does not seem feared. Après, il est fier, 'ow you say, proud? We all remember our premier bataille, and Rob-in, 'e remember 'e is doing good.'

'But what happened to him? He is not here, on the island?'
Jack asks, pleased to hear that his friend acquitted himself well,
but still anxious as to what has happened since then.

''E was 'ere to begin,' Gaston tells him. 'We all come 'ere after the bataille, with the ships of le roi. Pah!' he spits. 'Le roi, 'e
is not a man of 'is word. I am despise!'

'But Robin?' Jack persists.

'Ah oui, le petit. Il est ici for per'aps a week, two week, then
'e is go.'

'He is go? Go where? I mean, where has he gone? Was he going home? He never arrived. They're worried sick! Did he set off
from here, and have an accident, or something?'

Gaston looks puzzled. As Joubert translates, Jack finds it hard
to sit still, silently urging this old seaman to get to the point.

'Ah, oui, I am comprehend. Non, Rob-in is not go home. He is
go on bateau, boat, to A Coruña! 'Gaston' – that is me! – 'Gaston,'
'e say, 'I am never get chance encore. Now or never. I must go!''

Jack is dumbfounded. Robin survived the battle, was well
thought of, came back to the island with the Huguenot troops ...
and now has gone where?

'He's gone where, monsieur?'

Gaston and Paul Joubert are again conferring in rapid French
that Jack cannot follow. After a few moments, which to Jack feel
like hours, Joubert turns back to him.

'Jacques, Gaston is tell me your friend Rob-in, he is go to A
Coruña, in Espagne ...'

'Espagne?' Jack interrupts. 'You mean Spain? Why? Why in
God's name would he go to Spain?'

'Gaston is tell me the Rob-in is loving the sea. Per'aps not
the bataille, but the sail, the ships. He decide to learn sail, not
learn fight. He wish to be marin, marin-er? So, he is hear of new
place, yes, in Espagne, Spain. It is un ecole, a school, for boys of
the sea. He is go to be like apprentice, learn craft, yes?'

'God's teeth!'

Gaston looks puzzled now, and again says something to
Joubert in rapid French.

'Gaston say Rob-in is send message to home, to la maison de ses parents. He tell them he go to school to be marine. There is not time to go himself, or bateau will go without him. They did not get message?'

'No, they didn't!' Jack's mind works quickly. 'I wonder, you say he sent the message to the house?'

'Oui, Gaston say, he send writing to l'ancienne ambassade, the old embassy, en Surgères.'

'Oof!' Jack blows out a deep breath. 'That's why they never got it. They're not there. They're at the farm! Um … la famille, ils n'ont pas reçu le message … parce qu'ils ne sont pas en Surgères. Ils sont à la ferme, près de Marans!'

Gaston looks crestfallen, sorry to be the bearer of what turns out to be bad tidings.

'Désolé, Monsieur Jacques.'

'Ah non, Monsieur Gaston, don't worry. I will go and tell la famille. Ce n'est pas votre, um, fault. Merci pour votre histoire, et merci Paul. You'll tell le duc what happened?'

'Oui, bien sûr, of course. I will tell him now, if there is nothing also I can do for you? Non?'

For a third time, Gaston utters a long and, to Jack, incomprehensible sentence, and now it's Paul Joubert who blows out a long breath.

'Ah, Jacques, Gaston say I must be tell you also. The school in Espagne …'

'Yes? What is it?'

'I regret, Gaston is tell Rob-in, but he say it is no important. Espagne, it is like France is becoming, tout catholique. Gaston say they are not accept a boy who is French – well, French and Écossaise – and not catholique but protestant, who is come from Huguenot camp.'

Paul Joubert and Gaston escort a rather doleful Jack and his horse Thorn safely back to the ferry, trying vainly to persuade him that Robin will be fine and will come home soon – 'et nous serons hereux, we are happy, if 'e come again 'ere, to be wit' us!'

Damn and blast! Jack is thinking. What a mess! Of course Robin would send the message to Surgères, not the farm, and of course, the messenger would have known no better than to leave Robin's letter at the house. At least he sent a message, didn't just hie off without a by your leave – but that'll be small comfort to Rab and Jesette and Jeanne. I wonder why Rab didn't find out if a message was waiting at the townhouse? Ah, but no one can think of everything, and we all make mistakes …

Back in La Rochelle, Jack heads for the inn where he'd left Sam and Daan. The sun has set in a glorious array of gold and orange, edging the clouds with amber, already beginning to fade into indigo and purple. But all that Jack is aware of is his need for food, a bed for the night, and a halt to the tumult in his mind. He leads Thorn past the Eagle and spies Sam heading in his direction.

'Hey mate! Is work finished? Coming for a beer?'

Of course Sam is coming for a beer. With Thorn again settled in the stable, rubbed down, fed, watered, and safe for the night, the two men find a table by the bar, cupping their hands around their pots of ale.

'So what happened?' Sam is keen to know.

Quickly, Jack brings him up to date.

'You what? You met Soubise, and he was 'very pleasant'? What d'you mean, 'pleasant'! Ach, man, he's the terror of the nation! … A friend of your uncle? … Blow me down, Jack, who'd ever have thought it.'

All this is well and good, but after hearing about Robin's latest escapade, Sam agrees with Jack that there's nothing for it but he must go back to Rab. He must tell Rab about his son's typically impulsive decision to join a school for trainee mariners in Catholic Spain and explain about the misdirected message.

'I'll go first thing in the morning,' Jack says, gloomily. 'Best to get it over with. Nothing else I can do about it. Young Robin's gone.'

'Ach, at least they'll know what he's doing,' Sam tries to console him. 'Some news is better than no news, isn't it? But you'd best mind and be quick. Eagle's ready to launch again tomorrow, and then we'll be loading up. Flinty says he wants to sail the day after that. He's in such a fuss at this delay, I don't think he'll wait if you're not here.'

Great. That's all I need, the prospect of being stuck here.

'I'll be back,' he tells Sam, slightly grumpily. 'I've done my bit for Rab and Jesette. Never mind young Robin. It's time for me to get back to my own adventure now!'

CHAPTER SIX

'Jack! Jack, wake up! It's time to go!'

'Wha ... urghh ... oh!'

'You were well away, mate! Something about horses? And the waves?' says Sam, shaking his head with a smile. 'Come on. Daan's already gone, and I daren't wait, or Flinty'll be on my back all day.'

'Sorry!'

Jack scurries to get ready, wiping his bleary eyes, tying his bedroll back onto his pack, swilling the stale taste of beer out of his mouth. Rubbing his hands over his head, he tries to dismiss the strange images of his dream, the huge white creature rising from the sea foam, its mane a mass of menacing silver snakes whipping to and fro in the wind, waves as high as a house crashing down, pulling him under, swirling him down into darkness, towards the figure of a man, who holds a spear and laughs a cruel laugh.

At the quayside, Eagle is already back in the water and the finishing touches are being made to the repairs.

'Thanks for making space for me last night, Sam. And thank Daan for me, will you – 'though not for his snoring!' Jack says, as Sam darts off to join Daan and the others. Master Flint, keeping his usual strict eye on his ship and his crew, notices Jack. It's hard not to, as he delays his departure and stands idly, barely awake, next to Thorn. The horse is better rested than his rider, and better groomed, as well as having been fed and watered by the attentive stable boy at the auberge.

'Aha! Come back early to give a hand, have you Jack?' he says, slightly threateningly.

'Oh, er, no, Master, sorry. I'll be here tomorrow. Today I have to take my friend's horse back, and then ...'

'Ach, away with ye and yer excuses!' Master Flint still sounds stern, 'though he gives Jack what might pass for a smile. 'But mind ye're back at first light. We cannae wait for ye. We'll be heading out with the tide.'

'I'll be back!'

Jack swings himself into the saddle, raises a hand in farewell, and turns inland, watched by his envious crewmates.

All the way back to Marans, Jack is dreading how Rab, Jesette, Jon, and Jeanne will react to his news.

Why the devil couldn't I have found Robin safe and sound, or with a minor injury, or fallen desperately in love with some camp follower? Almost anything would be better than the truth, that he's gone off to join a mariners' school in Spain! God's teeth! Gaston was probably just being pessimistic, but what will he do if they didn't accept him? Come home with his tail between his legs, Jack fervently hopes, and marry yon fiery lass Jeanne with the long auburn hair. They could settle in La Rochelle, do a bit of trading like old Flinty does, if Robin really wants to spend time at sea. Perhaps they could persuade young Jon to develop the vineyards? There's always a demand for good wine … Och, but that's for them to decide, and Robin's got to come back from Spain first! As for me, all I can do is tell the family what I've been told, enjoy another night at the farm, and then … Ach no! How am I to get back to La Rochelle by first light if I stay the night at the Cosse place? It's nigh on a four-hour ride, so that means a good five-hour walk at the very least. Merde! There's nothing for it, but I'll have to go there and back today, cadge a bit of floor space from Sam and Daan again – or mebbe we'll be back in the hammocks and bunks on board. Ach, whatever. It's a bugger, but needs must. The most important thing is that I'll be on the Eagle when she leaves!

Jack's anxiety and frustration, and more than a little ill-feeling towards his childhood friend Robin, occupy his mind as the miles pass beneath Thorn's hooves. If he hadn't been in such a bad mood, he might even have enjoyed the ride on this fine spring day. He might have admired the flocks of geese, raised for

their skin and down, the white dots of sheep in the open mead-
ows, much prized for their soft wool. He might have spotted the
wild orchids in amongst the lush grass, heard the calls of the
sandpipers and warblers, and watched the eagles, circling high
above. But no. Today it's all wasted on him, and as his worries
spiral round and round in his head, his frowns get deeper, and
his face settles into a rare scowl.

Tou-tou is the first to hear him arrive and comes frolicking across
the farmyard, yapping with delight and wagging his tail. Jon,
as usual, follows close behind.

'Jack! We thought you might be back about now. You're just
in time for dinner! Oh, but no Robin …' Jon's voice trails off,
and his welcoming smile disappears.

'Sorry, Jon. I've got news, but p'rhaps best if I tell everyone
together?'

Jack slides off Thorn, strokes his glossy neck, and pats his
rump appreciatively.

'Thorn's been great, Jon. You chose well for me, thanks!'

'Oh, I'm glad. I'll see to him for you, shall I? You might like a
bit of a wash and a tidy up? You're smelling a bit high!'

The youngster's lack of tact at least provokes a laugh.

'Och, sorry! I can take a hint! All right, thanks, I'll do that.
See you inside.'

There's not much laughter at the dinner table. Now he's here,
Jack's veil of grumpiness has dissolved into the real underly-
ing anxiety of how they'll take his news. Rightly judging that
the first thing everyone will want to know about is Robin, Jack
saves his tale of meeting Soubise, and launches straight in.

'I'm so sorry,' he says. 'I wish I had better news. I wish I'd
been able to bring Robin back with me – or at least tell you he'll
be on his way soon. I can only tell you what I've been told. And
p'rhaps the most important news is that Robin's fine. The man
I spoke to, Gaston, he said Robin did very well at the battle, and
they'd be happy to have him back with them …'

'Oh!' Jeanne is quick on the uptake. 'You mean he's not there now, with the Huguenots?'

'No. As I say, he was at the battle with them, with this man Gaston, and Gaston said he was really good, really useful, although he's no fighter, and not much of a sailor yet! And that's the thing, you see. You know, and they could tell that Robin loves the sea and the ships – but of course, he's had no experience, no training, 'though they kept him busy with lots of other jobs. So when they all came back to the islands, apparently he decided that's what he wants to do, to learn about sailing, navigation and so on.'

'So?' Rab prompts, as they all sit on the edges of their seats, holding their breaths, waiting to hear whatever it is that Jack is building up to. Jon is cracking his fingers – 'Jon, please don't!' – and Jeanne is surreptitiously picking her nails.

'Aye, so … he's gone to a place called A Coruña, to a new school, to learn all these things, to become a proper sailor.'

Jack sits back with a sigh. He's told them the worst. Or he thinks he has.

'He's gone where?' Jesette asks, as Jeanne bursts into a flood of tears.

'To A Coruña, to the … now let me get this right, they did tell me … the, um, the Esc … Escuela de Much … Muchachos del Mar. That's it!'

If he was hoping for applause, Jack is disappointed. Jaws drop, foreheads crinkle into frowns, eyes blink in incomprehension.

'The Escuela de Muchachos del Mar?' Rab repeats, his tone incredulous. 'Is that what you said? Jack, are you sure? Lad, you know that's not French you're speaking – it's Spanish! Are you telling us that this place Robin's gone to, this Corona, did you say, it's in Spain?'

'I'm afraid so,' Jack admits. 'Yes, Robin's gone to Spain.'

Later, much later, when the exclamations, the shocked gasps, the volley of questions, and the tears, have died down, and everyone is dispiritedly pushing their food around their platters, trying to summon up the will to swallow at least something, and then abandoning the attempt, Jack is able to tell them his last piece of news.

'Um … Something else I need to tell you is that I've got to get back to La Rochelle. Eagle's in the water again, in the harbour. When I saw Master Flint this morning, he said she's leaving at first light. There's no way I could get back in time, so I'll have to go today, well, now really …'

'Oh Jack, no. I'm sorry to hear that,' Jesette says, looking sadder than ever. 'Oh dear … I wanted to sit down and talk with you properly, once this news about Robin has sunk in. It's been so long since we saw you, and you've been so good, to find out about Robin for us.'

'You're right, my love,' Rab agrees. 'And what I can't understand is why the wretched boy didn't let us know what he was doing!'

'Oh!' Jack realises what he's forgotten. 'I'm so sorry. Robin did let you know. Well, he tried to. I forgot to say. Gaston told me that Robin wrote a message for you before he left. He didn't have time to come himself, or he'd have missed the boat to Spain. Anyway, Gaston says Robin wrote this letter and sent the messenger with it to Surgères, to the old embassy. And I suppose it's still there at the house waiting for you. The messenger wouldn't have known any different.'

'Och, I'm glad to hear that Jack,' Rab says, looking momentarily happy. 'Well, at least, I'm glad Robin tried to let us know.' Then his face falls. 'Ach, but it's my own damn fault the message didn't reach us. If I hadn't been so determined to jump that hedge, I'd never have had that fall. If I hadn't had the fall, I wouldn't be laid up now. And if I wasn't laid up, we'd all have been back in town weeks ago. And why in God's name didn't I think to send someone to check at the house? Damn and blast!'

Jesette's eyebrows rise at Rab's language, but she says nothing. It's typical of her kind-hearted husband to blame himself, and she knows he'll chide himself for days. But Jon has been thinking about something else.

'Pa,' he says, 'isn't it market day in La Rochelle tomorrow?'

'Aye, it is.'

'So won't Monsieur Morel be taking the chickens and the eggs to sell? He's always whinging about having to leave in the middle of the night … Oh! I don't think I'm supposed to tell you that! … Um, anyway, couldn't Jack go with him, on the wagon?'

Rab is distracted from his self-mortification.

'Jon, you're a marvel. You've found the answer. Of course Jack could go with Morel. They could leave a bit early, just to be on the safe side. What d'you think, Jack? Would that suit you, get you back in time? They set the market up right on the quayside, at about six in the morning. Eagle won't go before then, will she?'

It's decided. Jack will leave with Monsieur Morel, and Jon is despatched to give the farm manager the no doubt unwelcome news that he'll need to be away by two in the morning. For the first time today, Jack begins to relax. Jesette and Jeanne, still looking pale and strained, take themselves off into the kitchen, startling the housekeeper out of her sneaky afternoon nap. They've decided that Jack must be sent off laden with food for the voyage. It gives them something to do, something to occupy them while their minds go round and round, absorbing the fact that Robin, beloved son and fiancé, has gone to Spain. Forgetting that Jack's an accomplished baker himself, and refusing his offer of help, they set about with a will. Soon both women are calmer, more composed, at least on the surface, and there is an array cooling on the window sill – chicken pie made with flaky puff pastry, semi-sweet brioche, a wholewheat loaf – all to be added to the food bag along with hard-boiled eggs, a round of soft cheese, and, of course, a flagon of wine.

With Jesette and Jeanne busy in the kitchen, and Jon helping load the cart ready for the next morning's trip to the market, Rab arranges himself again on the settle. Jack pulls up a chair alongside.

'Jack, we're not being very good hosts I'm afraid,' Rab confesses. 'We're so wrapped up in what's happening with Robin – and I'm stymied by this damn leg! But we're very glad you took the trouble to come and see us – and it was very good of you to go to the Huguenots for us. How was it? I didn't like to ask in front of the girls. I imagine it's pretty rough?'

'Well, actually,' Jack replies, rather smugly, 'I had no trouble at all. You see, I'd just got to the guard post by the ferry, and who d'you think turned up behind me?'

Rab shakes his head. He has no idea.

'Soubise himself! Yes, really! He wanted to know what I was doing there, of course, guessed I'd come off the Eagle, but when I said about Robin being the ambassador's grandson, and me being a Balfour, well, he couldn't have been more helpful. It was great,' Jack laughs, 'and he was so agreeable! Mind you, I wouldn't want to get on the wrong side of him …'

'Hang on,' Rab interrupts. 'I understand how Robin being Ambassador Cosse's grandson might be of benefit, but what d'you mean, when you said about you being a Balfour?'

'Ah well, apparently when my father and Uncle Will and Uncle Andrew were all in the army in Flanders, Soubise was there too, and he knew them. He said they were good men, that they fought hard.'

'Well, God bless my soul! Would you ever! Now that's a story you'll dine out on, my lad, for the rest of your life! Imagine that, Will and Andrew and Hendrie all knowing Soubise – and then you meeting him, just by chance. Fortune's favouring you, Jack, and I hope it stays that way!'

Rab pauses, wondering if Jack knows exactly how fortunate he's been.

'D'you know much about Soubise? No? Well …'

Rab tells Jack what he knows. Just four years ago, the French king had led an army against the Huguenots, capturing the town of Saumur and defeating Soubise at Saint-Jean-D'Angély, just to the south-east of Surgères.

'That was a bad time for everyone,' Rab says now. 'This whole area is predominantly Protestant, and there was a lot of suffering. Mind you, it was even worse down south, at Montauban and Nègrepelisse. There were terrible massacres in both those places, and the cities themselves were burnt to the ground. By God! And these are all supposed to be Christian people! It makes me sick, to be honest with you Jack. I don't see much future for any church if this is how they carry on. And did you know, Soubise's elder brother, Henri de Rohan, he's godfather to our king Charles! How's that for irony, eh?'

Rab pauses, his amusement banishing the expression of disgust and weariness from his face. But Jack is puzzled.

'Sorry, Rab, you said 'our king Charles'? You do mean our king? King James?'

'Ach, lad, of course, you won't have heard. It happened while you were at sea. King James is dead.'

Jack is shocked. 'What? The king's dead? King James?'

'Aye,' Rab replies. 'He died at the end of last month … twenty-seventh I think they said it was. He'd been ill for some time, so Charles and yon Buckingham – you know, King James's favourite? – they'd pretty much been holding the reins for some time. They say Buckingham was at his side when he died, God rest his soul. D'you know, I remember the day like yesterday, when the news came that Queen Elizabeth had died, and James was taking the English throne for Scotland. So excited we all were, 'though it didn't quite work out as we'd imagined … Aye, so we have a new king. And we'll soon get a new queen too.'

'Goodness! Is Charles getting married then? I thought that match with the Spanish princess – Anna-Marie was it? Something like that? – I thought that had failed.'

'Aye, you're right,' Rab confirms, 'the match with Marie-Anna did fail because the English parliament is so hostile both towards Catholics in general and Spain in particular!'

Jack frowns. 'And your Robin's heading off there, to Catholic Spain. Ach, I hope he's all right.'

'Thanks, Jack. We hope so too. But nothing we can do about it,' Rab says, grimacing. 'We'll have to trust that whoever's running this school takes Robin's enthusiasm into account! Damn and blast it to …' He shakes his head, fretting for his boy, then looks Jack in the eye.

'Ach don't mind me. I just feel so useless. But I was telling you, about Charles, the king I should say. So, word is that the new king's set on marrying one of the French princesses ...'

'But aren't they Catholic too?'

'Aye, that they are!' Rab manages a smile. 'So I reckon Charles is setting himself up for trouble, with yon English parliament. It's not like the old days, when the word of the king was law ... but I don't think Charles is minded that way. Ach, we'll have to wait and see. It's early days, but when you get back home, Jack, I think you'll find things are changing. But enough now about religion and the trouble it causes – or I should say the trouble people's pig-headed, self-righteous intolerance causes! Tell me, when you were having your cosy chat with your mate Soubise, did he mention someone else who served in the Dutch army under Nassau with him and the Balfour brothers? Someone by the name of René Descartes? No? Well, this Descartes, he's a bit of an engineer, a bit of a mathematician, one of these natural philosophers, you know, and I can see they'll be changing our whole future. It's fascinating ... What? You haven't heard about them? It's time you did! '

By the time the others join them in the salon for supper, Jack's head is reeling. As well as the bag of provisions to take with him, Rab has enthusiastically given him a copy of 'The Assayer', an essay published two years ago by Galileo and recently translated. Is it natural philosophy? mathematics? astronomy? Jack promises himself he'll read it soon, but it won't be tonight. He knows he'll be asleep as soon as his head hits the pillow, and hopefully with no time for any nightmares: there are only four hours before Monsieur Morel will be waking him.

CHAPTER SEVEN

The night is clear, cold, and still. Sitting next to Monsieur Morel as he drives the wagon along the lanes to La Rochelle, Jack cranes his neck and peers up at the stars. *Quite beautiful,* Jack thinks rather drowsily, the lurching of the cart's wheels into holes preventing him from falling back to sleep. *I must remember to read the book Rab gave me, by that Italian chap, what was his name? Galilee? Something like that. Rab said the Galilee person was a philosopher and a mathematician, who makes telescopes and thinks the Earth goes around the Sun. Well, I'm not sure about that, but I could do with one of those telescopes right now. There are so many stars ... and some seem to be clustered together, to make a great cloudy trail across the sky, like a silver river.*

'Monsieur Morel,' Jack says, 'celui-ci, c'est le Milky Way? Um ... le voie de lait?'

'Quoi? Ah, je comprends. Oui, c'est la voie lactée. C'est beaucoup d'étoiles, qui font une route dans le ciel. C'est belle, n'est ce pas?'

'Many stars, making a road in the sky ... Oui, monsieur. C'est très belle.'

'Je pense que le jeune Robin, il apprendra les étoiles. Les marins les utilisez pour la navigation, n'est-ce pas?'

'Um ... Sorry. You're saying Robin will learn about the stars for navigation? Yes, oui, je le pense. Je ne suis pas un mariner propre, je suis a baker, un boulanger!'

'Un boulanger?' Monsieur Morel pulls a face and nods, considering this. Deciding his passenger's French isn't up to much more by way of conversation, and being by nature a taciturn man, he lapses back into silence. The only sounds are the creak of the wheels, the soft thump of the horse's hooves, and the occasional squawk from their load of chickens when they hit a rut. Jostled together in their crates, surrounded by boxes of eggs, the hens are warm and snug under the tarred canvas cover that Monsieur Morel has secured against the off-chance of rain.

And so the miles pass. Gradually the stars disappear, and, as the wagon rolls into La Rochelle, the first faint glimmers of light are touching the clouds that have drifted across the sky. After the quietness of the journey, the town seems crowded and noisy, carts and wagons converging on the quayside, stall-holders setting out their wares, geese and more hens squawking, horses whinnying, men and women shouting and gossiping. The smells of animal dung, fresh fish from the night catch, and unwashed bodies, permeate the cool salty air. Spying Eagle still in the harbour, Jack breathes a sigh of relief.

Phew. She hasn't gone without me!

Scrambling hastily down, he neglects to offer Monsieur Morel any help with the hens and the eggs but does remember to thank him.

'Merci, Monsieur. I hope you sell everything ... I mean, j'espère que vous vendez tous les poulets et les œufs! Je dois, um, aller au bateau. Au revoir et merci encore!'

Morel waves him off, releases the horse from the wagon, and fastens her to one of the trees next to the water trough. He watches as Jack is swallowed up in the melee of mariners, busily loading the last of the cargo on board, under the eagle eye and the loud directions of the captain.

Ah, Morel thinks, *these boys and their adventures at sea ... Give me the land any day!*

He walks round to the back of his wagon and is surprised to notice that the heavy canvas is rumpled and loose in one corner.

That's odd. There was no wind on the way ... Ah, but not to worry. All the eggs and the chickens are still there, that's what matters!

Without giving it another thought, Morel sets about unloading, stacking the crates of hens on the ground, arranging a tempting display of eggs on the back of the cart. The sooner he sells them all, the sooner he can head home and catch up on some sleep.

'Jack Balfour! About time too!' Master Flint sounds typically gruff, anxious that they don't miss the morning tide and get back out to sea. Time lost is money lost, and with more and more routes opening up, merchant vessels are in stiff competition with each other.

'Sorry, Master. I came as quickly as I could. I'll lend a hand loading shall I?'

'If you'd be so kind!'

In fact, the only things remaining to be loaded are the provisions. Cookie has taken advantage of the market, stocking up on flour and meat, as well as several crates of Monsieur Morel's chickens and several boxes of his eggs. Too stout to manage them himself, one of the market lads is fetching and carrying for him. With everything stowed aboard, the gangplanks are lifted. Even Flinty manages a smile as Eagle slips away from the quayside with a cheer from the crew. As they pass between the Île de Ré and the Île d'Oléron, Jack, hoping no-one notices, snatches a moment to lean over the side and wave. He won't ever forget his short visit to the island and his encounter with Soubise. He doesn't suppose for a moment that Gaston or Paul Joubert are actually watching as the Eagle leaves, let alone Monsieur le Duc, but he likes to think perhaps they are.

After the stormy seas off Brittany, and the anxious passage in to La Rochelle, the next few hours seem very placid, the sea calm, just enough of a wind to keep them moving, heading west away from the coast and then turning south. Of the three youngsters, only Sam has been this way before. Daan's two voyages were both to the tideless Baltic, where the strong winds make for swift passage – providing they don't turn into gales and transform the voyage into a constant battle with the elements.

'Ach, but you wait,' Sam tells Daan and Jack. 'Bordeaux's a long way up the Gironde estuary, and it's not the easiest water to navigate. Frank and Master Flint'll have their work cut out, I dinnae mind telling you!'

'Why?' Jack asks. 'What's the problem?'

'Och, only the strong tidal currents, and about a million tiny islands to avoid, not to mention the spits between them where the estuary's silting up, that's all! It's nae a channel to try to navigate in the dark, however well you know it. So that'll be happening tomorrow I'm guessing – and I suggest we all keep out of Flinty's way until we're safe in to yon Port o' the Moon.'

'Yon what?' Jack asks.

'Port o' the Moon,' Sam repeats. 'It's what they call the dock in Bordeaux. It's on a bend, see, and they reckon it's like the crescent moon – la lunie, yon Frenchies would say.'

'Ah, mais oui, le port de la lune,' Jack says, showing off with his best accent, and getting thumped for his pains.

The following morning, however, with the mouth of the estuary within sight, Eagle sails blithely on southwards. Master Flint has decided to go straight on to Bilbao. Frank, the mate, has the job of telling the crew.

'Change of plan, lads. Cap'n says we'd best get to Bilbao soon as we can, offload there, pick up some bullion if we can, and mebbe some of this new stuff, sugar they call it. Then we'll head back to Bordeaux and fill her up with wine. The more wine, the more profit, eh? Keep an eye out for fog, all of ye. We don't want no more delays! And we'll be keeping in sight of the coast, so we avoid the worst of the winds and the swell. Biscay can be tricky even at this time of year.'

After his few days ashore, Jack soon settles back into the routine of the ship. He's already learnt how to haul a line, to tie knots that actually hold, and to climb the rigging. He's accustomed to working his four-hour watch and has learnt that it's best to stay below and out of the way the rest of the time: no one wants to trip over a novice, however well-intentioned they might be. But trying to sleep to a four-hour schedule doesn't feel at all natural, especially given that all hands could be called at any time, for anchoring or major sail changes. Eating to schedule still feels strange too. Jack's glad to have seen Monsieur Morel's chickens and eggs being brought aboard by the market lad. They'll make a welcome change from the dried peas, salt beef and interminable fish, not to mention the peculiar mixtures Cookie prepares in the brick-lined hearth in the galley. Brought up to the deck in buckets and doled out into wooden bowls by the cook's long-suffering assistant, it's not the most appetising fare, and Jack's glad of the weak ship's ale that gets passed round in a shared wooden tankard to wash it all down. Staving off slight feelings of homesickness for the mill, the bakery, and Nellie's plain cooking, Jack's also glad of his little stash of food that Jesette and Jeanne pressed on him. He's already surreptitiously eaten the chicken pie and has shared the cheese with Sam and Daan, with the promise of brioche whenever they can sneak away somewhere quiet to enjoy it. But on the whole, Jack's happy with his chosen lot, his adventure. He's mildly disappointed they're not heading for Bordeaux, to experience this estuary that Sam was talking about, and the Port of the Moon, fast becoming one of the busiest ports in the whole continent, but he consoles himself with the thought that they'll be calling in there on the way home. The flagon Jesette gave him won't last long, and he rather wants to sample some of the red wine of the region, having already enjoyed the white wines of Poitou-Charentes.

'So, Sam,' he asks his friend, 'have you been to this Bilbao place before as well?'

'Nae, sorry mate, I hav'nae,' Sam replies, 'but Gus was telling me it's the capital of the region and a pretty important port with its own merchant fleet. He says they used to pick up iron ore there. And ...'

Whatever else Gus has told Sam never gets relayed to Jack. A great screech is heard coming from the hold, followed by shouting.

'What on earth? ... That sounds like Cookie shouting his head off!'

Jack's right. A few moments later, Cookie himself makes a rare appearance on deck, dragging with him up the ladder a skinny lad looking terrified and trying to shake himself loose from Cookie's big meaty hands. Master Flint appears from the prow, frowning and severe.

'What the blazes is going on? Cookie, who's this ye've got?'

''tis a damn stowaway, Master, that's what. Found him huddled down in amongst the chicken cages.'

A stowaway! By God, thinks Jack, *I'm not sure if that's brave or foolish! But hang on, that jacket looks very familiar … It surely couldn't be Jon, could it? My Lord, now what?*

'Bring him to me!' demands Flinty. 'Ach, aren't ye the lad brought the chickens aboard, from the market in La Rochelle? Aye, I'm sure that was you.'

The boy cowers in front of Master Flint, keeping his head bowed, his eyes on the captain's boots.

'Nothing to say for yersel'? Cookie, what …'

As Master Flint speaks to him, Cookie is momentarily distracted and the boy, sensing his chance, wriggles out of his grasp and seems about to dash off – although goodness knows where to, on a ship.

'No you don't!' Daan, lithe and wiry, lunges towards the escaping figure, grabbing his belt and toppling over with him onto the deck. As the lad's cap falls off his head, his spiky auburn hair is revealed. He grabs for his cap – but too late. Jack has reached it first, has it in his hand … and seems frozen to the spot.

'God's teeth! Surely not! It can't be!'

CHAPTER EIGHT

Master Flint fixes Jack with a stony glare, as Daan hauls the stowaway to his feet and holds him tight.

'D'ye ken yon laddie, Jack? Speak up, man!'

Jack hesitates, recognising that the captain is already not in the best of moods. Does he really have to tell Flinty what he knows about this lad?

'Um, Master, I pray you, may we speak of this in private?'

'In private!' Flint roars. 'What the devil d'ye think ye ken that needs privacy?'

Angry, and fearing more delay, Flint nonetheless knows that Jack's a reliable lad, and that he's unlikely to beg for anything unless it was really important.

'Ach, blast ye, come away in if ye must. And fetch yon ragamuffin along with ye,' he says, indicating the stowaway, still cowering in Daan's strong grip.

As Flint strides off in the direction of his cabin, Jack holds out the lad's cap to him, which he hastily crams on.

'I'll take him from here, Daan, thanks.'

Clutching the lad's arm, Jack follows the captain, ignoring the malevolent glance from Cookie, but all too aware that the cook now has something else to hold against him.

Master Flint's cabin is small, but to Jack, accustomed to the crowded and smelly crew quarters down in the lower deck, it seems luxurious. There's a bed – *a real bed!* – a table and chair, a narrow closet built into the angle of the hull, and, best of all, a porthole. Flint stands, his back to the glass, hands fisted on his hips, waiting.

'Um …Thanks, Master Flint, for seeing us in private. I …'

'Us? Who's this us, eh? Ye and yon scumbag stowaway? What's he to ye? Ye'er paramour is he? Is that why ye were so keen to get out of the work in La Rochelle?' Flint sneers.

Now that's unfair, Jack thinks. *I'd have been glad to stay and work* … but he has the good sense not to say so.

'No, Master. Since you must know, he's my friend Robin's fiancée.'

'What the …?'

'Master Flint, allow me to present Mademoiselle Jeanne Rouane, fiancée of Robin Logan, who served with distinction at the Battle of Blavet under Soubise, and is the grandson of the late Nicolas Cosse, French Ambassador to Holyrood and Westminster.'

Jack has learnt the value of connections in high places. He nudges Jeanne, who lifts her chin, swipes off the grimy cap, and makes a low curtsey. In a corner of his mind, Jack is thinking that if it wasn't so serious it'd be funny. He purses his lips to prevent a smirk.

'Monsieur Flint,' Jeanne says. 'I am sorry for the trouble I cause you. I am need to get to Espagne, and Jack, 'e is say Eagle go Bilbao after Bordeaux, so I thought …'

Master Flint, gazing incredulously at this girl dressed in boy's clothes, her hair seemingly chopped off at random, finally gets his voice back.

'I don't give a fig for what you thought, Mam'selle. This is a trading ship, not a pleasure boat for passengers. Ye gods! A woman on board! I see now, young Jack, why ye insisted on privacy!'

Master Flint has in mind the superstitious belief shared by sailors everywhere, that it's unlucky to have women on board. The belief is that they distract the crew, and the gods of the sea become jealous and angry, creating storms and casting the ships into peril. Ships' figureheads, however, were often bare-breasted and female, since naked women were believed to calm the waters. Fortunately for Jeanne, Master Flint has no intention of testing this hypothesis. He sits down heavily on his chair.

'Jack, tell me what the hell is going on here. Who is this well-connected fiancé yon lass is seeking? And why Spain?'

Jack explains as briefly as he can. Master Flint is still unimpressed. He fixes Jeanne with a beady stare.

'Ye ken, lassie, that Bilbao is nowhere near A Coruña? And ye ken that yon mariners' place mebbe won't accept this Robin Logan? Ye're on a wild goose chase, lass … aye, and there's nought I can do about it. We're stuck with ye until Bilbao. Ye ken we'll have to put ye off there? Darn it, lass, ye've put me in a right fix.'

Master Flint is worried about what the crew's reaction will be when they discover there's a young woman on board. He's less concerned about what that young woman is going to do when they get to Bilbao. That's not his problem. Jack is ahead of him.

'Master, I'm thinking you wouldn't accept Jeanne as a paying passenger?'

The dour look on Flint's face tells him he's got that right.

'Well then, do the rest of the crew need to know she's a lass? If we can keep her out of the way of most of them, and Jeanne, if you're sensible and don't make a fuss about anything like needing your own privy or what have you, could we get away with it, d'you think? We could say she's Robin's younger brother Jon, come for an adventure to find Robin and bring him home. As to what happens in Bilbao, well … No, sorry Jeanne. I can't think that far ahead at the moment.'

'Oh, I will be walk to A Coruña,' Jeanne chips in, beginning to get a little of her usual confidence back. 'And oui, Jacques, je peux faire semblant, um … I am pretend to be Jon if it 'elp. I make no trouble. I 'ave la monnaie, capitaine …'

And so it is decided between the three of them. Jeanne, now known as Jon, will work alongside Jack, and keep as much away from anyone else as is possible.

'Frank can tell everyone I'm angry to have a stowaway on board,' Master Flint says, 'which is the truth! And he can warn them not to have anything to do with you until you leave us at Bilbao, or else they'll be answering to me. Jack, as you're the friend of this "Jon", it means some of the lads will try to give you a hard time. I'm sorry for that, but it's the best I can do.' He pauses, looking from one to another with a scowl. 'It's either that or the gangplank!'

'Oh mon Dieu!' Jeanne exclaims, struck with fear – until she sees a wry smile creep across the captain's face, and the hint of a twinkle in his eye. 'Ah, merci, Maître, capitaine. I am sorry for trouble to you. I will be like une souris, a mouse ...'

Fortunately for Jack and Jeanne, the crew are kept busy as Eagle is buffeted by the winds that grow ever stronger as they come in from the Atlantic. Staying out of everyone's way as much as possible, Jack concentrates on the menial tasks now assigned to him, and quite enjoys demonstrating some of his new skills to Jeanne – or Jon as he tries to think of her. The names are so similar, Jack's sure no one will notice if he slips up. Sam and Daan are of course curious, and despite the whole crew having been warned off by Frank, they gradually manoeuvre themselves closer in order to have a word with Jack.

'Jack, mate! So this is your friend's brother?'

'Aye, Sam, this is Jea ... Jon. Crazy boy's taken it into his head to follow Robin to A Coruña. Says he left a note for their parents and hid on the wagon that brought me back to La Rochelle. Huh! The mad fool!' Jack says, glowering at 'Jon'.

'Sorry. Sorry, Jacques,' Jeanne says.

I know I've been told to say as little as possible, she thinks, but *I can't say nothing at all!*

'I 'ave to find Robin ...'

Just as Sam and Daan are both wondering why this Jon has such a funny accent – and that his voice hasn't even broken yet – Frank spots them.

'Oi! You two! Get yerselves over here and back to work! No free passages on this ship, thank you very much!' he calls, looking straight at Jeanne, who wisely ducks her head and gets back to tying the knots Jack is teaching her – or rather, back to tangling the strands of hemp into a complete mess.

That night, with Jeanne tucked away on Jack's bedroll underneath his hammock, sleep is elusive. This was not the adventure Jack wanted or imagined, to be hampered by a lass he barely knows, to be pretending she's a boy, and preventing anyone else from finding out the truth, to be covering for her the whole time, not daring to relax his guard. No, this is neither what he dreamed of nor hoped for.

But it is what it is, Jack thinks, resignedly, *and I suppose that no-one can say it's not just a bit exciting, certainly more so than the daily grind at the mill back home! And at least Jeanne doesn't seem to suffer from sea-sickness, like I did at first. But what to do next? If these winds keep up, Eagle should reach Bilbao the day after tomorrow, and I know that Master Flint means what he said. Jeanne will have to leave. She must be mad! To think she can just walk to A Coruña, on the north-west coast of Spain? That's all the way across the whole country! By God, it must be what, nigh on four hundred miles.*

Jack's luck stays with him and Jeanne throughout the next day.
'I am enjoy this,' Jeanne whispers to him in a rare moment on their own. 'I am see what my Robin is liking … and you boys, you are have so much more freedom than girls. I am think …'
'Hush!' Jack shushes her. 'You'll give the game away, and we're nearly there now.'
'Oh! When are we arrive?'
'Tomorrow morning and …Now go swab the deck and then swill out those buckets as I told you, Jon,' Jack's voice suddenly changes as he hears someone coming. 'And mind and do it properly this time!'

As Bilbao comes into sight, the sun shining down on the ancient city walls, the rooftops, and the Nervión river, Jack fails to feel the relief he expected.

Yes, Jeanne will be leaving ... but there's not a hope in hell that I can let her leave alone. Damn the woman!

Jack's heart sinks. He goes to find the Master before he can change his mind. Flint's reaction is much as expected.

'You're what, Jack Balfour? Here I am, giving a novice a rare place on my ship, and not only d'ye swan off in La Rochelle and then bring a girl on board – och, I ken,' Flinty admits, in the face of Jack's protestations, 'ye didnae bring her y'sen, but it amounts to the same thing ... And now, by the Life, ye're telling me ye're leaving? Just when I was seeing the makings of a useful seaman in ye. Ach, Jack.'

The master pauses, seeing the conflict of desire and duty chasing one another across Jack's face.

'Master, I'm sorry. I don't want to leave. You know I don't. It's been great, all of it. But you do see that I can't just abandon Jea ... um, Jon. I can't let her, I mean ... Och you know he's a she! So, I can't let her wander about in Spain on her own. I'd never be able to live with myself.'

Master Flint relents, letting out the avuncular soul that he keeps hidden behind his usual gruff exterior. He sighs, claps Jack on the back and leaves his hand on his shoulder, heavy and comforting.

'Aye, lad, I ken. Ye're in a right fix, and I cannae argue agin ye. I wish ye well lad – but mind now and help us offload afore ye go!'

CHAPTER NINE

As Eagle docks at the port of Bilbao, Jack has his pack ready, the bedroll once again tied on at the base. His heart is full of regret: regret to be leaving the ship and his shipmates, regret that he may never again have the chance to explore Bilbao or Bordeaux, regret that his conscience won't let him abandon Jeanne, and regret that he didn't bring his other pair of boots. Jeanne, to her credit, has tried to talk him out of coming with her to A Coruña –

'I can do this, Jacques,' she has repeatedly told him. 'I am never meaning to bring you with me!' – and now she tries to give him one last chance to duck out.

'Jacques, please stop and think again. If you are come with me, it is take long time, long walk, to where my Robin is. And then we do not know how to come home again. You tell us all before, at the farm, you are having three months and then work again at mill in Leith. But you may not be home then ...'

'Ach, Jeanne, I know all this!' Jack's voice is hard, as he struggles to contain his emotions. 'D'you not think it's been going round and round in my head? Yes, I may lose my work at the mill, but no, I cannot let you go alone. I've written letters to Miller MacMoran and to my Uncle Will, to explain what's happened. Sam says he'll deliver them for me when Eagle gets back to Leith, and that Flinty's sure to find someone willing to work their passage in my place. So that's the best I can do, and that's all there is to it. Now please, stop mithering me, all right?'

'Yes, Jacques. I am sorry,' Jeanne replies, with unusual meekness, not understanding all his words, but realising with some relief that he has made his own decision.

'Come on then. You're still Jon for now, remember? I've already spoken to Sam and Daan, but we need to give a hand offloading all the cargo.'

Dumping Jack's pack by one of the bitts on the quayside, he and Jeanne join their crewmates, already beginning to pass down the crates and boxes, to empty the skips of coal, the sacks of fleeces. Master Flint spies them.

'Jack! Aye, and Jon – get yerselves over here!'

Fearing that Flinty has changed his mind about letting them go, Jack and Jeanne glance anxiously at each other as they go over to the captain, but their fears are unfounded.

'I've had enough of the both of ye!' Flint says, loud enough for the rest of the crew to hear. 'Get on yer way now, and don't let me be seeing you again!'

Dropping his voice to a whisper, his mouth curling into a rare smile, he says, 'Good luck to ye both. Jack, I'm sorry to lose ye. If ye ever need work, come to me – but leave yon lassies at home, ye ken!'

'Thanks, Flinty! I mean, Master!' Jack replies with a barely concealed grin.

Master Flint cuffs his head lightly and turns back to the crew, while Jack, raising his hand in farewell, and with Jeanne silent at his side, shoulders his pack and walks away.

Striding along the coast path, Jack's mind gradually begins to settle. It was a wrench leaving Eagle, and he knows he'll never forget a moment of the whole voyage.

Ach, but for now, Jack decides, I must set all that behind me. For all that she's been pretty damn reckless, stowing away like that, Jeanne didn't mean any real harm. And Flinty letting us off early, that's a great bonus. The sooner we get to A Coruña and find Robin the better!

'Are you all right, Jeanne?' He glances at his companion, trudging silently at his side.

'Oh, Jacques, oui, all is well. We are arrive in Spain, and we are walk to Robin, and the sun, it is shine.'

'I don't suppose,' Jack asks a few minutes later, 'that you have any idea of the way?'

'Oh!' Jeanne's hand flies to her mouth, open in sudden realisation. 'Non! Je ne connais pas le chemin … Ah,' she shrugs, 'but I think we walk all along the sea – how you say, the coast? – and then we are arrive.'

'Hmm. That's sort of what I thought too,' Jack admits. 'Let's hope we're right. There's no one to ask anyway!'

The path is deserted, and they don't see anyone else until, around midday, they reach a small fishing village. A few stallholders are still packing away their remaining goods from the morning market. Jack plonks himself down on a great rock by the beach, pulls off his boot to examine and pad a blister, then munches on the salt beef and slightly stale bannock that they brought with them. Jeanne has gone to investigate the remaining stalls, and is soon deep in conversation, pointing and gesticulating. Jack notices her hand reaching into the pocket slung around her waist.

'Oh God,' he thinks, ungenerously. *'What's she buying? It'll be me that ends up carrying it in my pack, and it's full enough already!'*

When Jeanne returns, he's abashed to see that in fact she's bought her own small pack and bedroll, as well as a flagon of some kind of local ale, smoked fish, and a loaf.

'Oh! Well done,' he greets her, shuffling along the boulder to make room. 'Here, sit down and have something to eat.'

As the days pass, Jack and Jeanne settle into a routine, rising with the sun, taking a break at midday to eat, check their sore feet, and wipe their sweaty foreheads. Then they walk again until sunset, usually finding a bed for the night in one of the sleepy villages along the coast, occasionally resorting to the shelter of an abandoned shed or a hedge. They walk alongside marshes, across beaches, sometimes turning inland to find a ford or a bridge over the many small rivers running down to the sea. They see very few people, just the villagers, the market traders, and the innkeepers. Sometimes they are passed by people riding donkeys, whom they take to be farm labourers. Sometimes they are hailed:

'¡Hola! Buen camino!'

'Buen what?' they shrug, shake their heads, smile and wave, and walk on.

Turning inland, around the Bay of Santander, they're almost surprised by the noise and bustle of the town and are tempted to take a detour, to explore the streets that sprawl beneath the watchful gaze of whoever is in the castle on the hill. But no, they press on, keeping the sea on their right. On their left, the pleasant landscape is a patchwork of green pastures and forest, gradually rising into the tallest mountains they have ever seen. The weather is kind, and Jack and Jeanne enjoy the fresh air after the cramped ship, feeling their muscles getting stronger, their skin browner, their blisters healing. They sleep soundly each night, tired from their daily walk, and they don't talk much, but their silence is comfortable. At one of the markets, Jeanne has bought herself a shift and a plain gown, and, while Jack is buying food, she goes into the sea, to splash herself as clean as she can, put on her new clothes, and rinse the breeches, tunic and jacket she took from Jon's clothes chest back at the farm. Dried by the sun, stiff from the saltwater, she stuffs them into her pack and feels more like herself again, although her hair is still shorter even than most boys'.

About a week after they left Eagle at Bilbao, they're forced to walk further inland, due to the numerous estuaries and the lack of a coast path. After a couple more days, they cross over yet another river, follow the path as it turns north towards the coast, and arrive in quite a large town. There's a new looking dock, with a few merchant ships in amongst the fishing boats.

'Oh, it's good to see the sea again,' Jeanne enthuses. 'Now I feel I know where I am!'

Jack laughs. 'Yes, I know what you mean,' he says, while feeling again a nostalgia for his days on Eagle. 'It's early yet, but shall we stop here, have a bit of a rest, find somewhere to stay the night?'

'Oh, Jacques, oui! That is a good idea!'

There are plenty of inns – 'tabernas' they are learning to call them – along the quayside. Choosing one at random, Jack pays for two rooms and orders a meal while Jeanne takes one of the tables next to an open window, overlooking the harbour. *Goodness, but it's nice to sit down!*

She eases her feet out of her boots and watches idly as a group of people disembark from one of the ships. They have packs on their backs and staffs in their hands. *Of course,* Jeanne thinks, *les bâtons! We must get some.*

'Regardez, Jacques,' she says, as he joins her, with a flagon of the wine they are becoming accustomed to, and the promise of their habitual evening meal – fish stew – to come. 'Look, les marcheurs, walkers like us.'

As they sip their wine and gaze out of the window, an argument breaks out among the people who've just come off the ship. Too far away to hear the words, Jack and Jeanne can hear the shouting and the clash of staffs, they can see the raised fists and the way two young men hold another back from retaliating when he's struck. It's all over very quickly. As two of the men stride away, one of the remaining three spots the tavern and Jeanne at the window, points, and says something to his companions.

'Looks like they're coming in here,' Jack says, and he's right.

As the three newcomers crowd their way into the little bar, one of them, the one who was hit and had to be held back, is a little unsteady on his feet and bashes into Jack.

'Tá brón orm, mo chara! Um … lo siento, amigo.'

He doesn't sound Spanish, Jack thinks.

'Nae worries, mate,' he says, testing what the reaction will be.

'Oh, you're not Spanish,' the man says in surprise. 'You're English?'

'Scottish. Well, I'm Scottish. My lady here is French. And you?'

The newcomer introduces himself as Liam. He, Pádraig, and Brendan are from Ireland – 'Skibbereen, d'you know it? No? Ah, no matter' – and their ship, he tells them, should have put in at Ferrol, but the sea was too rough. Coming in here at Gijón was a safer bet.

'Those other two – I think you'll have seen the argument just now?' Liam says. 'Well, they were angry, blamed us for not insisting to the captain that we go on to Ferrol. Stupid fools!' Liam looks disgusted. 'It makes our way longer, but why does that matter? The saint will still be there for us whenever we arrive, God rest his soul.'

'The saint?' Jeanne asks, as Liam perches on a stool at the next table, and his two friends join him. 'What saint?'

'Saint James, of course! Are you not pilgrims too? We thought you must be, by the look of you – no offence, ma'am.'

Jack and Jeanne are still puzzled.

'I'm sorry. I don't think we know what you're talking about.'

What Liam and Pádraig and Brendan are talking about, and continue to do so at great length and with great enthusiasm, is the pilgrimage to Santiago de Compostela. Known in English as the Way of Saint James, Jack and Jeanne learn that there is a network of pilgrim routes dating back several centuries, leading to the shrine where the remains of the former fisherman turned apostle, Saint James the Great, are buried.

'King Herod had James killed, and his body was carried by boat from Jerusalem here to Spain, where he is buried. The ship was piloted by an angel, but it was hit by a storm, and when it landed it was covered in scallops,' Brendan tells them. 'That's why the scallop shell is the symbol for the pilgrimage – and we've been told they're mighty useful for scooping up water at the fountains along the way! While we're here, we'll get one each. Shall we get them for you too? P'rhaps you can get your staffs as well. You'll come along with us, won't you?'

Liam and Pádraig nod encouragingly – 'Yes, join us!' – but Jack and Jeanne aren't sure.

'I don't know if we're going the same way,' Jack tells their new friends, being honest, but also a little wary after the scene on the quayside. 'We were planning to keep walking along the coast path until we get to A Coruña. That's where my friend, Jeanne's fiancé is. We've come to find him.'

Liam is undaunted. 'Ach, but you'd have to come inland anyway. There's no path all the way round the coast. If you came with us as far as Melide, where several of the paths meet, you can turn off and head up to A Coruña, and we'll go on to Santiago.' Seeing Jack and Jeanne glancing uncertainly at each other, Liam hesitates.

'It's up to you. But like I say, there is no coast path, and a bit of company might be safer than just the two of you.'

'Ah,' Jeanne says, 'this is good idea, yes, Jacques. We are safe to here, but per'aps five is better than two? But Li-am, the way you go, it is to les petits villages, oui? There are beds at night?'

Liam laughs. 'Yes, Mam'selle Jeanne. There are some villages and some taverns like this one, but also there are hospitals, um, not for sick people but like hostels, auberges, you know, run by the church 'specially for us pilgrims. My brother, he was here four years ago, for the Holy Year, that's how come I know all this stuff about it. He said these hospitals are good – simple, but clean beds and enough food. They like you to go to mass 'though. Is that a problem?'

'Pas pour mois,' Jeanne replies. 'Not for me, I am Catholique. C'est curieux. I am knowing of les pèlerinages, pil-grim-ages, to Rome for Saint Pierre, and Jerusalem for le Seigneur Jésus, and Cologne for les Trois Rois, but I am not knowing of this. I am not know why I not know! But any-way, I am good for the Mass, but Jacques …'

'I'm open-minded!' Jack says with a grin, abandoning his reservations. 'All right, Liam, you're on. We'll come with you, as far as Melide.'

Jeanne, eating less than the men, finishes her meal first, and asks the question that's been puzzling her.

'May I ask, why you are become pèlerins, pil-grims? Is it nor-mal in Irlande?'

'Ah, no. Times are changing, Mam'selle …'

'Please, you are call me Jeanne.'

'Jeanne. In the old days, many people went on pilgrimages, but since the schism and the coming of the English to Ireland, there are fewer of us who are able to follow the old way. Ach, they'd rather follow the king and Calvin than the Holy Father.'

'But you three,' Jeanne persists, 'you do this for adventure, or for pen-ance, or for blessing?'

'All three, I think. But rest assured Mam … Jeanne … we're doing this of our own free will, not for punishment!'

'What d'you mean?' Jack asks, startled.

'Ah, you see, sometimes people are sent to do them for their crimes. I can't say whether or not it works,' Liam laughs, 'but you need to be careful. Not everyone's motives are pure!'

CHAPTER TEN

Once they've finished their meal – Jack has somehow ended up ordering and paying for three more plates of fish stew and a second flagon of wine – the three men decide to take a walk around the town. Jack has agreed to keep an eye on their packs, while he enjoys another glass of wine and finally gets down to reading the book Rab gave him, the essay by the Galilee man, whose name turns out to be Galileo Galilei.

Funny old name, Jack thinks.

Jeanne excused herself a little while ago and has gone to her room for a rest.

'I have des règles … You know, Jacques, each month?'

Jack, brought up with his four brothers first by their grandmother and then by their spinster aunt and bachelor uncle, actually hasn't a clue.

'Oh, right, well yes, whatever. You have a rest. I'll sit here and read.'

He digs the book out of his pack, unearthing at the same time his flageolet and realising he's hardly played it since leaving home; just a couple of evenings on Eagle, to entertain Sam and Daan and the other lads.

Mebbe I'll give it a go this evening, he thinks. *I wonder if the Irishers have their pipes or anything with them?*

Soon, he's absorbed. 'The Assayer' is written in the form of a letter to the new Pope Urban, and Galileo describes himself as 'mathematician and philosopher to the Grand Duke of Tuscany'.

Hang on! Jack racks his brain. *That sounds familiar. Yes, of course! Uncle Michael, God rest his soul, was the Scottish ambassador to the Grand Duke of Tuscany, Cosimo de Medici. Goodness! Uncle Michael must've known this Galileo chap. How interesting! I wonder what they thought of each other, Michael so conservative, and Galileo apparently such a radical?*

Jack smiles at the thought and returns to the slim volume. He's still there a couple of hours later. Dusk is falling and the first star is shining bright. Liam, Pádraig, and Brendan return to the tavern, but Jack hardly notices them for a few moments.

'You're deep into that book,' Liam comments. 'Something good?'

Jack emerges from the complexities of Galileo's arguments, shaking his head to clear his mind and focus again on where he is.

'Oof! I don't know about good, as such,' he replies, 'but it's fascinating stuff. It's about how we should use mathematics, rather than philosophy, to ... what does he call it, 'read the book of nature'. I think that means, you know, to see God's revelation in the actual world, not just in the Bible. Something like that! I'm not sure I fully understand it.' Jack is sounding earnest, but the three men, settling at the table, tankards in hand, laugh.

'That's a bit high-falutin' for us, Jack lad!' Pádraig says, with a slight sneer.

'Oh, well, for me too really. Rab gave it to me – he's Jeanne's father-in-law, or he soon will be.'

'Ah, this elusive fiancé ... Yes, we were wondering about him, and about what you're doing with the lass. Mind, she's looks more like a lad than a lass! Keeping her warm, are you, for your missing mate?'

It takes a moment for Jack to realise what Pádraig is suggesting.

'God's teeth, of course not! That's a disgusting suggestion, and ...'

Pádraig lifts his hands, palms towards Jack, warding off his anger, as Brendan thwacks his arm hard.

'Sorry, Jack, mate,' Liam says, 'Pádraig's got a mind like a midden. Let's leave him here and sit outside, shall we?'

'Sorry,' Pádraig mumbles and takes a swig of his ale as Jack and Liam get up from the table.

'I'll stay here with this bastard,' Brendan says, scowling at Pádraig, 'and keep an eye on him, all right?'

As Jack steps outside with Liam, he misses the glance that passes between the three men, the almost imperceptible nods, the glints in their eyes.

Outside the evening is cool, the sky clear. Jack and Liam perch on a bench.

'No hard feelings, Jack, eh?' Liam says, after a few minutes of silence. 'Brendan will make sure Pádraig minds himself with you and the lass. He can't control his mouth – or much else – when he's had a few, you know.'

Slightly mollified, and not wanting to seem naive or petty-minded, Jack points up at the sky.

'The man who wrote my book,' he says, realising he's left it inside on the table, 'he makes a thing called a telescope, to look at the stars and the moon and such. I'd love to try that. They say it brings them nearer, so you can see them properly.'

'I don't know about that,' Liam replies, 'but we've a story in Ireland, about the Milky Way. Bealach no Bó Finne we call it, the Way of the White Cow.'

Jack listens idly, still curdling inside from Pádraig's comment, as Liam tells the legend of how the Milky Way is a heavenly reflection of the River Boyne, created by the goddess Boann, and the place where the hero Fionn mac Cumhail captured Fiontán, the Salmon of Knowledge. It seems to Jack to be a complicated story, about hazelnuts and burnt thumbs, and he doesn't really care, but he lets Liam ramble on.

'... and so Fionn became the leader of the Fianna, the warrior bands.'

Liam glances at Jack, who is still staring into the sky.

'Of course, here, on the camino,' he says, 'they tell how the Milky Way guides the pilgrims along the way and was formed from the dust kicked into the air by all the people on their way to Compostela. That means 'field of stars' you know,' he ends proudly.

Jack stirs, puts down his glass.

'I think I'll take a wee walk, if you don't mind,' he tells Liam, 'just along the dock and back. I don't know why, but watching the stars is making me miss the sea!'

At the far end of the quayside, Jack turns inland and wanders through the labyrinth of alleys that make up the little town of Gijón. Candles flicker in some of the windows, the occasional burst of laughter breaks the silence, and somewhere someone is playing something that sounds a bit like a fiddle, but isn't, and there's an insistent rhythmic clacking that quickens Jack's pulse and stirs his energy.

I'm in Spain, he thinks, as if discovering the fact for the first time. *Spain under the stars, with strange music and ...*

Crack! Everything disappears in a bright blackness.

'Are you all right?'

Concerned voices pierce the dark, stabbing into Jack's consciousness.

'Ow! My head! What happened? Where ... Who are you?'

Two faces are peering down at him, where he lies sprawled on the rough ground of the alley.

'We were just walking back to our room, almost fell over you! Looks like you've been coshed. D'you not remember?'

No. Jack remembers nothing, just a strain of music at the edge of his mind and a burst of starlight.

'D'you think you can stand if we help you?'

'Thanks.'

As strong arms raise him up, Jack's stomach heaves – 'Sorry!' – and he vomits copiously into the gutter. The acrid stench of the semi-digested fish stew hits him in the face and he reels away. His rescuers are hovering at a slight distance.

'Better now? Where are you staying? We'll walk you back.'

'Oh!' Jack feels for his pocket, his purse. 'I've been robbed! My purse, my pocket, they're gone.'

'Aye, lad. There are some ruffians about. There were three of them on our boat, Irishers, sent over to do the pilgrimage for their crimes. Ach, I reckon all that does is shift their thieving elsewhere, and ...'

'Three Irishers? Was it you who had a bit of a brawl earlier, when you came off the boat?'

'Aye. You saw that did you?'

'We did. They said you were angry not to be taken on to Ferrol.'

The man gives a half-laugh. 'No, lad. That's nonsense. The boat was always bound here, to Gijón. What happened was that yon tall one, calls himself Liam, had his hand on my pocket, and a knife, ready to cut the cord. Idris here saw him, stopped him. Ach, nobbut trouble all the way across. Thank God they're gone.'

'Gone with my purse, I reckon,' Jack says. 'Oh God, and I left my pack with them at the inn!'

Idris and Kai walk with Jack back to the tavern on the quayside, opposite the boat they'd arrived on earlier that day. It's as they feared. The Irish men are gone and with them Jack's pack. The innkeeper is regretful but had thought they were all friends. He didn't pay much attention when the three Irishmen left. How long ago? Oh, perhaps treinta minutos, una hora? Jack slumps on a stool, still feeling sick, and with a thumping headache. He'd been taken in good and proper, taken for a fool, acted like a fool, trusting complete strangers.

'Damn and blast them to hell!' he curses them, knowing there's nothing he can do.

'I'm so sorry,' Idris says. 'Can we do anything? We're staying just around the corner. Shall we come back in the morning, to make sure you're all right? That was a nasty blow to the head you took, and it's still bleeding. You'll need to be careful.'

Jack touches his head – 'Ouch!' – his hand coming away sticky with blood.

'Thank you, you're very kind. Ach, but I must check upstairs on my companion!' Jack suddenly remembers Jeanne. 'God's teeth, if they've touched her ...'

The proprietor picks up Jack's sudden concern, his attempt to stagger to the stairs. 'Los irlandeses no tenían habitación, no se les permitía subir las escaleras.Y tu amiga la señora no ha bajado en toda la noche.'

'What is he saying?' Jack asks. 'I don't understand Spanish.'

'Ah, he says the Irish didn't have a room, so they weren't allowed up, and your lady has not come down,' Kai says confidently, explaining 'I've been here several times, for the pilgrimage, so I've picked up a bit of Spanish.'

'I'm impressed,' Jack says, trying to smile. 'Um, gracias Señor!' he says to the proprietor, then he turns to Kai and Idris.

'I'm sure Jeanne's fine, but I'd better check on her, and then I think I need to lie down. I'd love to say I'll treat you to breakfast, but I've no money now – oh God, and they took my flageolet, and my book, and the lace for Aunt Elspeth ...'

Seeing his distress, Jack's two rescuers encourage him to go and rest.

'We'll come back in the morning to see how you are, you and your lady,' they assure him. 'Don't worry about breakfast. You try and sleep – but give your head and your hands a good wash first, to get rid of the dirt and the blood, eh?'

Making his way gingerly along the upstairs corridor, Jack taps on Jeanne's door.

'Jeanne, are you awake?' he calls softly.

The door opens a crack, and Jeanne replies, 'Oui, I am wake ... Oh Jacques! Que s'est-il passé? Ta tête!'

Hustling him into her room, sitting him on the bed, Jeanne fetches a cloth and dips it into the bowl of now just warm water brought earlier by the maid for her wash. Gradually she soaks away the caked mixture of mud and blood from Jack's head, untangles his matted hair. The wound itself is not too bad – 'Oh God, but it's sore!' – but the bruising on his jaw where he fell is already turning reddish-purple. Jack explains, and Jeanne is horrified.

'Those men? Those Irish men – they did this? Oh mon Dieu, they are méchant, wicked! I 'ate them!'

'But the worst thing is, Jeanne, they stole my purse and my pack. I've nothing left!'

To his shame, Jack's lower lip begins to wobble. Jeanne, putting down the soiled cloth, wraps a towel around his head and takes him in her arms, soothing him like a mother to a child. He'd like to resist, to be manly and strong, but the pain overwhelms his anger and pride.

'Jacques, Jacques it is being all right, we be all right. Oh, your poor poor head, but you are good and strong, hush now, hush, all is well.'

'But Jeanne,' Jack's voice comes out in hiccups, 'what are we to do?'

'We are to go on,' Jeanne tells him, determinedly. 'We walk, walk, walk, to A Coruña to my Robin. I 'ave my monnaie, my pack, my rouleau de lit. We are manage. Do not be worry. Is adventure, yes? Hush now, rest, rest and sleep, sleep and heal …'

True to their word, Idris and Kai return to the little tavern the next morning, carrying their packs, staffs in their hands, and scallop shells around their necks. Jack and Jeanne are just finishing their breakfast. Jeanne's pack and bedroll are ready. They've decided to move on, even if Jack will be slower than before. They've had enough of Gijón. Jack introduces the two Welshmen, explaining that he and Jeanne are on their way to A Coruña, 'to meet up with Jeanne's fiancé,' he says optimistically.

'Which way are you going?'

'Well, originally we'd planned to walk along the coast path. Then those thieves told us there is no path, and said we should go with them to somewhere called Melide, where the ways divide,' Jack replies. 'That's what they said, but I don't suppose they ever intended it to happen, damn them. We were sitting ducks!'

'Well, they were right about there not being a path,' Kai tells them. 'You'll need to come inland. I daresay you're not feeling very trusting right now, but if you want to walk along with us, you're welcome, isn't that right, Idris?'

His companion nods. 'Of course. There's safety in numbers. We can just keep each other in sight if that'd be more comfortable for you.'

'Oh, oui, merci,' Jeanne says. 'But we will not be vite, um, fast, aujourd'hui, to-day.'

'That's all right. We'll just be getting into our stride today. We're heading for Orviedo. That's about six, seven hours.'

'I can do that,' Jack says, sounding more convincing than he feels. Everything aches.

Perhaps walking will ease it, he hopes. *Kill or cure, eh?*

'But les irlandais …' Jeanne suddenly looks anxious and pale, 'they are not going this way, you think? I am afraid to see them – afraid and furieuse, both!'

'I think they'll be long gone. They've Jack's money in their pockets now … but if we do see them, they'll regret it!'

Now it's decided, Jeanne discreetly passes Jack her purse – 'Oh, yes, I'll just …' – but the proprietor waves him away.

'Lamento tu molestia. Los brek-fass, es gratis para ti, free for you! Buen camino!'

CHAPTER ELEVEN

It's a breezy morning. Idris and Kai hang back, to let Jack and Jeanne get a hundred yards or so in front of them. The path leads uphill out of the little town, and the walkers have their backs to the sea. Every step feels like hard work for Jack, his joints stiff from crashing down onto the cobbles when he was attacked, the bruising on his jaw tender, the split on his head no longer bleeding, but 'It's bloody sore!' he tells Jeanne with a grimace. They pause briefly to buy themselves staffs.

'Buen camino!' the friendly shopkeeper says, coming outside to wave them on their way, broom in hand to sweep away some rubbish the breeze is swirling outside her doorway. Jeanne has already set off, pushing her way up the hill, when out of the corner of his eye, Jack sees something familiar.

'Madam, stop!' he startles the shopkeeper. 'Please, let me see!'

Jeanne comes back, as Jack crouches down by the pile of rubbish.

'Jeanne, look, it's the pages of my book, the one Rab gave me, by the Galilee man. The bastards! They've torn the back off ... and here, look, here's my flageolet ...'

The mouthpiece is cracked, but the rest of the little flute is intact. Jack is on his knees now, mindless of his bruises, ferreting through the little pile of leaves and dirt, catching the pages of his book before the wind whips them away again, passing them to Jeanne. Kai and Idris have caught up with them, and the shopkeeper's husband has emerged, along with several neighbours, who stand in a cluster, chattering and pointing.

'What's all this? Things from your pack?' Kai asks, taking the pages from Jeanne and smoothing them out. 'These can be fastened together again, lad. They're still readable, and mebbe you can glue a bit of bone to your flute?'

'Señor, ¿esto es suyo?'

One of the neighbour's children has been scrambling about in the ditch, and now holds out a grimy strip of fabric. It flutters in the breeze as he passes it to Jack.

'Oh, it's the lace! The lace I bought in Bruges for Aunt Elspeth!'

Jack clutches it to his chest, as if it were a rare and precious piece of treasure, his eyes filling with tears.

'Thank you! Gracias!'

Nothing else can be found. Jack's knife, spoon, scissors are gone, along, of course, with the purse he kept in his pack.

And that had most of my money in it, he thinks, with a surge of anger and despair. *If I ever see hide or hair of those thieves …*

Jeanne has put the pages, the lace, and the flute, carefully into her pack, and shoulders it now.

'Jack, viens! Come! We must go on.'

Raging inside, blaming himself, plotting all manner of revenge, Jack follows Jeanne's lead as the miles separate them from the coast, and the track rises and takes them into the green hills. He looks back just once, but beyond the shepherding figures of Idris and Kai, Gijón is no longer visible, and the sea has disappeared. Stopping only at a couple of wayside fountains, to drink, eat, and disappear behind convenient bushes, they reach Oviedo by dusk.

'This is one of the most important pilgrimage sites on the camino,' Idris tells the others. 'The cathedral is full of relics brought back from the Holy Land at the time of the Crusades, including …' he pauses for effect, 'the Sudarium, the cloth that was wrapped around the head of the Lord after his crucifixion!'

'Goodness!' Jeanne and Jack do their best to respond with enthusiasm, although actually, the only things that both of them are interested in right now are a meal and a bed.

'And it was from Oviedo that King Alfonso set out to verify the remains of Saint James – so really,' Idris continues, bubbling with enthusiasm, 'this is where the camino, the pilgrim route, truly begins. And here we are! We can go and see the Sudarium, now, tonight!'

'Oui, here we are!' Jeanne repeats. 'But Jack, he must rest, or else he will not walk any more of the camino to-morrow!'

When they leave the town of Oviedo, the little pilgrim band heads west. They climb up hills, trudge alongside farmland and woodland, walk through the tiny villages that straggle along the route, and gaze in awe at the views of the Cantabrian Mountains. Without knowing it, they have passed into Galicia, an area which, until the arrival of the Romans, was occupied by the ancient Celtic tribe, the Gallaeci. Occasionally they are passed by other people, walking or riding on donkeys, and Jack feels guilty for slowing Kai and Idris down. Even more occasionally they overtake other pilgrims, some barefoot, some shuffling on their knees, yet others walking a few paces and then prostrating themselves, rising and walking another few paces, and again lying face down on the ground, arms outstretched. Finally, a week after leaving Gijón, and having endured cold winds and heavy showers of rain, they arrive in Lugo. The oldest town of the region, Lugo is sited on a hill, surrounded by three rivers, and completely encircled by high walls, interspersed with many tall towers. Kai tells them the bits he remembers of what he was told when he came this way before.

'They say that Lugo was the pagan god of light, and there was a sacred grove here in his honour. That's how it got its name of course. But then the Romans came and began mining for gold – yes, really, there is gold here! And then Julius Caesar himself landed in A Coruña – that's where you're going isn't it? – and came on here with all his troops.'

It's ancient history, Jack has been thinking, *and slightly dull*, but the mention of A Coruña acts like a trigger for his flagging motivation, sparking him out of his lethargy.

Yes, of course, he realises, as if waking from a dream, *that's what this is all about, this long long walk – to get to A Coruña, find Robin, and somehow bring him home. It's odd, but I'd almost forgot-*

ten. I'd almost forgotten everything except the daily routine of rise and eat, walk, rest and eat, walk, shelter from the rain, walk, eat and sleep. Must be that knock to my head, he thinks, grinning wryly. *I feel like I've been in a trance, just walking, walking, walking forever!*

'Jeanne, are you all right? I'm sorry. I've not been very good company for you.'

She turns and recognises there's something different about his tone of voice and the expression on his face. She smiles with relief.

'Ah, Jacques, it is all right, I am all right. You have been, how do you say, préoccupé? Your mind, it was somewhere else all this time. I am think it is from the hurt to your head and to your soul. You need time. But you are here now?'

He laughs, the best sound Jeanne has heard for days.

'Yes, I'm here now. I'm back – and I suddenly feel well.'

Two days later, full of energy and with their good humour fully restored, Jack and Jeanne emerge from a shadowy forest and arrive at Melide. Several groups of pilgrims are already here, those who overtook them along the way and others who have come along a different route from the border with France. Everyone seems friendly, sharing their experiences over a carafe or two of wine, washing down the speciality of the region – octopus – and discussing the final stage of the walk and the arrival in Santiago. Idris and Kai have soon caught up with them, and the four spend one last night together, lodging at the monastery of Saint Francis attached to the Sancti Spiritus church. The following morning, they say their farewells. The Welshmen are relieved that Jack seems better, to have overcome the physical and mental damage caused by his assault, while Jack and Jeanne are grateful for their sensitive concern.

'I shall miss them,' Jeanne says, watching them as they catch up with another group of pilgrims and are swallowed up, indistinguishable in the crowd.

'Yes, they're good men, and I'm glad you weren't entirely alone while I was recovering myself. Ach, but now I feel like a new man!

All this walking may have given us sore feet and weather-beaten faces, but it's straightened out a few knots in my mind!'

'Bien!' Jeanne replies. 'Good!'

She doesn't really know what he means, but does that matter? No. She grins at Jack.

'You begin again to enjoy this adventure?'

'Yes, oui, sí!' he replies, returning her grin. 'So what, I was robbed by some scoundrels? It happens every day, everywhere. I'd rather be me than them, however much gold they've got in their pockets!'

Jack's high spirits are infectious. Chatting and laughing, he and Jeanne reach Ponte Carreira by mid-afternoon. It's a lovely bright sunny day. Even 'though they've been told that they should stop here for the night – 'There's nothing else until Carral!' – the unusually level path tempts them, and they decide to press on. After a mile or so they cross the site of a quarry, where a couple of workmen are packing up their tools.

'¡Hola! ¿Estás perdido?'

'¡Hola!' Jack replies, then mutters to Jeanne, 'I'm getting the hang of this!'

Jeanne is not impressed. She's too busy coughing and batting away the clouds of stone dust. Undeterred, Jack continues.

'Señores, este el camino … um … Carral?'

'Carral? Sí, pero es un largo camino, quizás cinco horas. Deberías volver con nosotros a Ponte Carreira para pasar la noche.'

Ach, what?

'Do you speak English?' Jack asks, not very hopefully, but Jeanne has learnt a few phrases from Kai.

'¿Habla usted Inglés o Francés?' she asks.

The man who spoke shakes his head, then holds up his hand, the fingers splayed out, and tries again. 'Carral, cinco horas.' Then he points back the way they have come, now putting his hands together and resting his cheek on them. 'Ponte Carreira. La noche.'

'Oh, gracias. Entiendo.'

'What?' Jack asks her. 'What's he saying? Five something and sleep?'

'Yes. I think he says Carral is five hours and we should go back to Ponte Carreira to sleep.'

'Ach, damn it. Is there nowhere else? It seems a shame to go backwards.'

Jeanne tries to remember a few more of the words she has just learnt. She points the way she and Jack were heading.

'Un albergue? Una hostal?'

Now the two workmen are conferring, and the other one speaks.

'Allí está la ermita de San Amado.'

'¿Ermita? Ermitage? Gracias!' she calls to the men and then turns to Jack. 'There is un ermitage, a hermitage. We can stay there I think.'

The hermitage of Saint Amaro is tiny, just a single-roomed, white-washed building set back from the path. But the doors are unlocked and there is a fountain.

'Will this do?' Jack asks, 'Or would you rather go back?'

'Non, c'est bien, this will do.'

Jeanne sets about creating a very temporary home in the empty shell, unrolling their thin mattresses – they bought one for Jack in Lugo – shaking out and re-folding their spare clothes for pillows, arranging their food on the single stool.

'I am forget this place,' she tells Jack. 'Idris, he tell it me. He say Saint Amaro was a pil-grim, un pénitent, who is go to Santiago and then he make the places for other pil-grims to sleep, like here, and also un hôpital pour lépreux ...' She pretends to scratch her skin and contorts her fingers to show Jack what she means.

'Oh, bad skin, um, leprosy?'

'Oui, exactement.'

'Ach, I don't know about leprosy, but d'you think sleeping here will get rid of the fleas?'

'Quoi? Ah non! Jack, non, pas les puces!'

By way of penance for his teasing, Jack spends some time collecting twigs and branches, piling them together to make a little fire, where they sit munching their supper as the sky darkens from blue to grey to indigo to black, the stars brightening into fiery dots. But for the rest of the night, whenever she's half awake, Jeanne can feel herself itching, and before they leave in the morning, while she picks a posy of wildflowers to leave at the shrine, she insists Jack follows her example and has a thorough wash in the icy water of the fountain.

From the hermitage, it's a relatively short walk to Carral – only fifteen miles –their last stop before they reach A Coruña. Jack sniffs the air appreciatively as they approach the main square, oblivious to the magnificent views of the surrounding countryside.

'Delicious!' he declares. 'Best smell in the world!'

'Quoi? What are you smell?'

'Bread! Good bread!'

Following his nose, Jack is soon at the panadería, the bakery. The shopkeeper is talking excitably with another woman, who is trying to make space for two loaves of bread in her already bulging basket. As Jack and Jeanne enter, their conversation falters.

'Buenas tardes, señor, señorita, ¿cómo puedo ayudarla? ¿Sois peregrinos? Aquí tengo un poco de pan que puedes tener gratis.'

'Buenas tardes,' Jack repeats, rightly guessing it means 'good afternoon,' as Jeanne reaches into her pocket for their purse.

'No, no, es gratis' the shopkeeper insists, shaking her head. 'Peregrinos, free bread.'

'Ach, nae, gracias,' Jack says. 'We are not pilgrims, non peregrinos. We are walkers, on our way to ...'

The other customer looks around at the sound of Jack's voice.

'Ooh!'

As her basket falls to the floor, oranges spill out, rolling away towards the door, where Jeanne busies herself gathering them up again. The woman has gone as pale as wood ash.

'Hendrie? It cannot be! No, no, Hendrie está muerto ... and you are too young. Who are you?'

CHAPTER TWELVE

'Sara, ¿estás bien? ¿Quienes son esas personas?' the baker asks, breaking the silence.

'Oh Vera, lo siento. Este joven se parece a alguien que conocí hace mucho tiempo.'

As the baker raises her eyebrows with a slightly sardonic smile, the customer turns to Jack and Jeanne.

'Forgive me. You give me a shock! I am say to Vera, you look like someone I know long long time ago.'

Jack isn't sure whether this is good or bad.

'What was his name, my lady? You said 'Hendrie'? That was my father's name.'

'Your father? I am not believe this … Your father, he is Hendrie Balfour?'

'Yes.'

The woman turns even paler and looks slightly sick. Jeanne, quickly dumping the oranges back in her basket and putting it safely on the floor, grabs the stool that's been holding the door open and gently pushes the woman onto it. Jack is standing like a statue, lost for words.

'Madame, vous dites que vous connaissiez le père, um … you say you know the padre de Jacques?' Jeanne asks.

'Oh, this is, you are, Jacobo? Here, here in Carral? Are you look for me, for Conn?'

Questioned directly, Jack comes back to life.

'My lady, how could I look for you? I don't know who you are! And you say you knew my father? Where? When? How …'

Vera, the baker, despite her fascination with whatever it is that's happening in her shop, is even more interested in closing up and going home. She pretends for a moment to tidy up the already tidy counter, holding out the last of the day's batch of loaves to Jeanne, having decided she's the most sensible person there, apart from herself.

'Señorita, es tiempo de ir a casa.'

'Um ...' Jeanne is not quite sure what she's being told, but Vera's words break the spell holding Sara and Jack.

'Oh, lo siento, Vera. Te traeré la loción mañana ...' She adds another sentence in Spanish, unintelligible to Jack and Jeanne, who glance at each other, puzzled and confused.

'I am say to Vera that I bring her lotion tomorrow, but now I go home with you and find what is happen,' she explains, hustling them out of the bakery, calling back to Vera, '¡Te lo contaré todo mañana! I tell you tomorrow!'

Sara has evidently recovered from her initial shock. As they all hesitate in the market square, she smiles at Jack.

'You are Jacobo, yes? Jacobo Balfour, son of Hendrie and Geillis?'

'Yes, I am Jack, but ...'

'And this is ... ?' She looks at Jeanne.

'I am Jeanne Rouane. I am to marry Jacques' friend, Robin Logan. He is in A Coruña, so ...'

'Robin Logan? He is family to Rab Logan, Missy's dear friend?'

'Oui,' Jeanne replies, feeling completely muddled. 'Rab is the father of my Robin.'

'Oh, Rab's son, you are to be marry, yes? Oh, please, come home with me and we can talk. Conn will be there. Oh, I never imagined ... It is not far. Please, will you come?'

Jack isn't quite sure what to make of all this. The name Conn seems familiar, but he can't quite place it. And this woman, this Sara, she knew his parents, and Aunt Missy and Rab? But who is she? Jeanne sees his confusion.

'Jacques,' she says to him quickly in an undertone, 'let us go with this lady. We must find out who she is and what is her connexion to your family, non?'

As he nods, Jeanne turns to Sara.

'Gracias, señora, we come to your home.'

Nothing more is said as they follow Sara away from the centre of the little town, although from Sara's face it seems she is about to explode if they don't speak soon and sort everything out. After walking for less than five minutes, Sara stops outside a square stone house, roofed with terracotta tiles. Pots of geraniums are in flower on the deep window ledges. They can hear the cackle of chickens and the gurgle of a nearby stream.

'Bienvenido al El Hogar!' Sarah says, beaming. 'Bienvenue, welcome to Le Foyer, The Hearth!' She pushes the door open. 'Come in, please.'

Jack and Jeanne, becoming more intrigued than ever, dump their packs in the passageway and follow Sara to the back of the house. They find themselves in a large kitchen, where a man is putting logs on the fire. The delicious smell of wood smoke mingles with that of some kind of stew simmering in a huge pot.

'Conn, estoy de vuelta, I am back,' Sara says, as the man straightens and turns around, 'and we have invitadas, guests!'

As she puts her basket on the enormous wooden table that dominates the room, he comes over and gives her a kiss.

'So I see. Welcome to you both.' He reaches out to shake their hands. 'Have you come far?'

As Jeanne and Jack come further into the room, light falls on them from the far window. As Jack returns Conn's handshake, the older man stares at him, puzzled.

'Oh! Have you stayed with us before, young sir? I think I almost recognise you, but I can't quite ...'

Sara cannot contain herself any longer. She claps her hands together in delight.

'Conn, this is el hijo, the son, of Hendrie Balfour! Yes! Hendrie from Leuven. It is Jacobo! ... and with him, la nuera of Rab Logan, his daughter-in-law, Jeanne. They were in the panadería ...'

'Well, I never did! Hendrie's son Jack. And Rab's daughter-in-law? By God, how amazing. Come and sit down, both of you, and tell us all about it and why you're here!'

As Sara unpacks her basket, Conn pulls out some chairs for them at the table. As he does so, they hear the front door open and slam shut, the sound of footsteps going upstairs, talking and laughter.

'You have family? Or other guests here?' Jeanne asks. 'We do not want to be, how you say, in the ways?'

Conn laughs. He laughs a lot, a rich ringing sound. He is a happy man these days.

'No,' he says, 'not family, but we almost always have guests here. This is a hostel, for the pilgrims, you know? We offer them supper and a bed for the night and then breakfast before they set off again. We've met a lot of extraordinary people! Is that what you're doing, walking the camino?'

Sara joins them at the table.

'No, Conn,' she says. 'They say to Vera they are not peregrinos. But ...'

'Forgive me,' Jack breaks in, 'but I don't know who you are.'

'Oh, Jacobo,' Sara's hand flies to her mouth and she looks dismayed, 'I am so sorry. I am not introduce myself or Conn. Lo siento, I am sorry. I am Sara Benjumeda and this is mi esposo, hus-band, Conn Canamraghe.'

Jack looks blank. 'I am, I mean, we are, happy to meet you, and thank you for your welcome ... but I still don't know who you are. You mentioned Leuven. I know my father was based there when he was in the army of the Dutch Republic. Is that where you knew him?'

'Aye, lad, that's right,' Conn says, frowning slightly at Sara. Catching sight of this, Jeanne wonders why, but keeps silent. 'We were in Leuven at the same time as your father Hendrie, and his brothers Andrew and Will. Hendrie was wounded and Will took him back to Scotland. Then Andrew and Anna left to get married and have their baby. Soon after that, we had to leave too. It wasn't safe for Sara and her sister, and not easy for me either, being Catholic in a Protestant stronghold. We followed Hendrie and ended up with Will and Missy and Walter in Fife. I was planning to go back to Ireland ...'

'Ah oui, bien sûr, of course, that is your accent!' Jeanne bursts out, smiling. 'I was perplexe. But it is different sounding from some voleurs, some méchant thieves we met in Gijón. They hitted Jacques and stole his pack and all his money!'

'Oh! This is terrible,' Sara exclaims. 'You are good now?'

'Thank you, yes, I'm better ... So,' Jack refuses to be diverted, still focussing on working out who these kind people are. '... you knew my father and then you stayed with Aunt Missy at Pittendreich House. Is that it?'

This time Jack catches the worried look that passes between Sara and Conn.

'Is there something else?' he asks, suspicion beginning to stir. 'Why did you follow my father all that way?'

'Ach, Jack lad, it was Sara's sister who decided to follow your pa, and we went with her. Then afterwards, I went off travelling ...' Conn pauses and unconsciously touches the pendant that hangs round his neck. 'And Sara,' he continues, 'stayed with Missy, didn't you?'

Sara nods. 'Yes, I was learning about the remedios, how to make with las plantas y hierbas, and ...'

'No, sorry, you said your sister? I'm beginning to think ... Who is your sister?'

'Maria,' Sara replies, looking mortified. 'My sister is Maria.'

In an instant, Jack is on his feet, his chair crashing backwards onto the floor, his face at first pale, then flushing with anger.

'Maria? My father's mistress? Dear God!'

The other three are now also on their feet, Sara clutching Conn's arm, as Jack strides to the door.

'Jeanne, we must go.' He looks at Sara and Conn. 'I'm sorry. I don't mean to offend you, but we're leaving.'

If Jack was expecting Jeanne to follow him meekly, he's about to be disappointed. 'Jacques,' she says, standing her ground by the table, 'I am see that you are upset, but I am not know why. Please, we sit again and you say what it is, and then if we must, then we go. Mais pas comme ça, not like this, non.'

Jeanne's tone of voice – one that will brook no dissent – catches Jack off guard, his hasty exit interrupted.

Damn, damn, damn and blast.

He turns to Jeanne.

'Jeanne, you don't know what happened … my mother's death … and then afterwards …'

She moves towards him now and takes his hand. 'Come back, Jacques. Tell me, tell us, what this is about, and then we are to decide. Please?'

Through the fog of shock and anger, Jack allows himself to be brought back to the table. Conn rights his chair and then reaches for a jug of wine, pouring it into four glasses. As they all gradually settle, allowing their breathing to return to normal and their pulse rates to steady, the story emerges. It is all new to Jeanne. Jack's father Hendrie, while stationed in Leuven for several years, had an affaire with Sara's elder sister Maria. Neither she nor Jack's mother Geillis knew about the other and Hendrie divided his time between the two. The details of the complicated story rather go over Jeanne's head, but she gets the gist. Hendrie returned to Scotland, and Maria followed him there, accompanied, as they had already said, by Sara and Conn. Geillis died giving birth to Jack's youngest brother Harry. Jack's elder brother Billy had learnt of his father's affaire and he had refused, on behalf of all the children, to have anything further to do with Hendrie. Jack and his brothers were brought up by Geillis' foster-mother Ma Mayne. When she died, Billy inherited her cottage, and the other four brothers moved to Hawkhill to live with their spinster aunt and bachelor uncle, Elspeth and Will.

'We never speak of our father,' Jack says. 'He lied to both Ma and to your sister,' he nods at Sara.

'But you know Jack,' Conn says, 'it was no more Maria's fault than it was your mother's. They both loved your pa … Yes, I know that may be hard to hear,' he continues, as Jack begins to protest, 'but it's the truth. And Hendrie took advantage of that. The army was his first love, aye, perhaps his only love.' He laughs again, but wryly this time. 'God's teeth! I remember when I first heard about it all. I was as angry then as you are now! And I took it out on Will, poor fellow, stuck in the middle of it all. Good man 'though. I liked him a lot.'

Jack is silent for a moment, taking in what Conn has said, recognising the truth of it, liking him for liking Will.

'You know my father died?' he eventually says, 'and six months after that, his … well, she, Maria, your sister … she had a son, Robert.'

'Oh!' Sara is astonished. 'I am not know this! Hendrie is dead and Maria has baby?' She frowns, working it out in her head. 'No, not baby. He must be big boy now … I am aunt!'

Seeing Jack and Jeanne's confused expressions, she explains.

'After Maria is with Hendrie in Edin Burgh, I am in Fife with Missy. I am her aprendiz, um … apprentice? I stay two years. Oh, and it was happy time, except per'aps for missing Conn, just a little …' Sara laughs, as Conn glints at her, then gives way to a grin. 'Anyway, I decide to come home to Espagna. Not to where I am born, León, because of the trouble there … No, but that is otra historia, another story. So I come here to Carral. It is good place, quiet, then busy when the pil-grims come. I make new life, but I have no news of Maria. Four years before now, Conn is arrive here. It is Año Santo, Holy Year, so he is peregrino. It is ten years since we are meeting, and I am not wait for him in las Escocia while he makes his viages and his discoveries …' Sara smiles and Conn takes her hand '… but he find me, and so we marry. This is all. And now you. Please, stay with us a little? I know you are angry and hurt, but we like to know you …'

'And besides,' Conn butts in with a smile at his wife, 'there's a fish stew ready for eating, and Sara always makes far more than we need for the guests we have!' He lifts his wife's hand, still clasped in his own, and kisses it. 'It's up to you, but you're welcome here – and we'd like to know why – I mean, why you're here?'

Exhausted by the emotion of their unexpected encounter, their difficult conversation, aware of the evening drawing in, and guessing Jeanne's wishes, Jack slowly nods.

'Thank you. If you're sure, then we will stay. I'm sorry for, well, you know, being hasty. We do have our own stories to tell,' he goes on, as Sara pats his arm and Jeanne smiles with relief, '… and I love a good fish stew.'

CHAPTER THIRTEEN

Jack is the last one downstairs the next morning. The group of six pilgrims whom they met last evening have long since eaten and gone, and Jeanne is helping Sara with the dishes.

'Buenas días, Jacobo. Come, there is plenty for you on the table.'

She chatters on, as he piles food on his plate.

'It is good, hearing your stories last evening. I am not imagine we have a friend of el duque de Soubise with us – nor a valiente stowaway,' she teases Jeanne, who blushes and smirks. 'I am glad you are stay here today with me, Jeanne, and let los hombres go to A Coruña to find Robin. Conn, he is in stable, get horses ready for you, Jacobo.'

'Oh! Um … Shall I go and help?' Jack manages to say, his mouth already full of tortilla, savouring new tastes and textures. Sara is an experimental cook, eschewing the purely traditional, and adding to the onions and eggs what she had already told Jeanne are 'pimientos, maíz, y patatas del nuevo mundo – from the new world!'

'No, no, you eat. Is good, yes? Try this!'

Sara pours hot brown liquid into a mug, and Jack takes a sip.

'Och, it's sweet! What is it?'

Jeanne joins him at the table, holding out her half-empty mug for a top-up.

'C'est délicieux, non?'

'Oui, um … yes, it is. Sweet but sharp too?' Jack says, taking another swig of the strange drink.

'Esto es chocolate,' Sara tells them. 'It is chocolate. It is beans, come from the New World, and mix with miel, honey you say, vainilla y pimienta, hot pepper, just a little. You are like it?'

'Mmm … It's different,' Jack replies tactfully, while thinking that a tankard of small beer wouldn't go amiss. 'I've heard of a new drink in England,' he says. 'It's called coffee. Do you know about that?'

Sara shakes her head, no, but Jeanne is familiar with it.

'Ah oui,' she says, wiping away a chocolate moustache from her upper lip. 'I have had this café. It is made from seeds, burnt and then …' Not knowing the word, Jeanne mimes, her left hand forming the shape of a container, her right fist clenched and moving as if crushing and grinding something.

'Milled? Ground?'

'Oui, exactement, moulu. It is strong, a little bitter? I am think it come from les Turcs, the Turkish people, the mussalmans.'

'Ah, is this so? My antepasados, um, ancests? back long time ago, they are mussalmans. I am think they not from Turkey, but from África,' Sara tells them. 'Once, all of España, it is mussalman, muslim, but then the christianos, they are coming back, and they do not allow other creencias, other religiones. Is sad.' Sara pulls a resigned face. 'I am think all creencias, all belief, should be free.'

As Sara is speaking, Conn has come into the kitchen through the scullery, blinking as his eyes adjust to the cool, shady room after the bright sunshine outside.

'Morning, Jack!' He claps Jack on the back, almost making him choke on his last mouthful of tortilla. 'Are you ready? I've put what we'll need in the saddlebags.'

'Gaah …' Jack gulps and coughs, 'yes, thanks, I'll just …' He swills down the last of his chocolate. Strange stuff.

'Buen chico! Come on then. It's a good three or four hours to A Coruña. Sara, Jeanne, we may be back today, but I doubt it, so don't expect us until tomorrow. We'll stay with Lorenzo and Bella if we can. You'll be all right?'

Reassured that they'll be fine and having once again quelled Jeanne's impulse to go with them – 'No, Jeanne, it'll be the same as the Île de Ré, and no place for women!' – Conn and Jack swing themselves up into the saddles and, with a final wave, head north.

They're not in a hurry, and Jack surprises himself by enjoying being on horseback again, after so much walking. Then he had mostly watched his feet, but now the little bit of extra height gives a much better vantage point for viewing the lush green of the countryside, the eagles circling high above in the blue sky, the occasional pilgrims in twos and threes heading in the opposite direction. Jack is hardly aware that he has a broad smile on his ruddy face, and he certainly doesn't care that his mop of dark hair is getting even more tangled by the light wind. He's forgotten, of course, to bring his cap. This is the final stretch of the long journey to A Coruña. He's looking forward to seeing Robin again, although he's likely to give the younger lad a mouthful for causing all this trouble, and Jeanne – agreeable girl 'though she is – will be happy, and off his back, at last. Thinking of Jeanne, Jack's mind wanders to another girl, back in Leith ... and he's startled when Conn, having noticed the faraway look in Jack's eyes, interrupts his daydream.

'Penny for your thoughts?'

'What? Och, mebbe not worth a penny, Conn! I was just thinking, um ... how pleased Jeanne will be when we bring yon Robin back to her. And ...'

Conn rather doubts this was really what was in Jack's mind, but he runs with it for now.

'Aye, but it's good of you to do this for them, giving up your own escapade, your voyage on the Eagle. D'you think you'll go back to sea, work your passage back home after this?'

'Ach, I dinnae ken yet,' Jack replies, lapsing into a broader Scots accent now that he doesn't have to ensure Jeanne's understanding. 'I did enjoy it on the ship – I felt more like me, you know, without the family and everyone whose known me forever all around ... but I hav'nae really thought that far yet. Once we've got Robin safely back, then I'll work it out.'

'I do know what you mean, lad, but they'll be missing you at home,' Conn suggests. 'D'you not feel homesick at all?'

'Homesick? Nae!' Jack says, dismissing the moments when in fact he has missed the mill and the bakery and yes, even his family. Realising he's not being entirely truthful, he admits,

'Well, there's been times since I left the ship when I've missed Uncle Will … and then being with Jeanne all this time, it's, um …'

Jack flushes and stutters to a halt.

'Someone else you're missing?' Conn asks, with a twinkle in his eye.

Jack looks back at him, slightly warily. This is something he's not spoken about with anyone.

Aye, he thinks, *but Conn's not likely to be one to gossip – and who would he tell anyway?*

'Well … there is someone, a lass …'

Conn bites his lips together to prevent his laughter from bubbling out.

Surprise, surprise!

'A lass,' he manages to say, straight-faced. 'Really? Someone special?'

Jack sighs. 'Mebbe so. Her name's Jennet, Jennet Tullois, but I call her Jennie. She's young yet, just sixteen …'

'Ach, lad, Sara was sixteen when I first met her, and I must've been about your age, mebbe even a wee bit older.'

'Really? Och, well, the thing is, some of Jennie's people – their estate's between Cupar and Saint Andrews, but they have a house in Edinburgh – anyway, they're planning to go to the colonies, in the Americas. Virginia, Jennie says. Her brother Claud's definitely going. And she could go with him, but I don't know if she will.'

'Well, if there's nothing to stop her going, why shouldn't she?' Conn asks provocatively, but then seeing Jack's usually bright face turn despondent, he takes pity on him.

'But mebbe you could be the reason for her not to go, eh?'

They ride on in silence for a while, as Jack mulls this over in his mind.

Conn might be right. So far nothing's been said, nothing definite. It's been more a sense of possibility, of something in the air between us. And that's not enough to stop my Jennie leaving … oh, my Jennie.

Jack realises this is how he thinks of her, as his, and he as hers. In that moment, it's as if the whole world is turning up-side-down, making his stomach churn. He feels quite giddy, and shakes his head, as if he's been submerged and is coming up for air.

My Jennie, yes! Ach, now I have something, someone to go back for, if she'll have me?

Conn's been watching Jack out of the corner of his eye. He senses a change in the lad and remembers a similar cusp of fate with Sara all those years ago, when the whole world had seemed to hold its breath. As he opens his mouth to speak, a burst of singing disturbs them, and the moment is lost. A little way ahead, quite a large group of pilgrims has clustered around one of the wayside shrines. Not wishing to disturb them, Conn and Jack slow their horses and pass quietly by, but Conn has recognised the Irish hymn they're singing and he hums it softly under his breath. Once they're out of earshot, Jack comments on the haunting tune, thinking perhaps he could play it on his flageolet, once he's mended it.

'That's the Fáeth Fiada,' Conn tells him. 'It's a prayer Saint Patrick himself sang when an ambush had been laid to prevent him reaching Tara. Because of his prayer, he and his followers seemed to his enemies to be wild deer, and they let them go by. Miracle or magic, eh?' Conn says with a laugh. 'Or myth?'

'And you know this hymn? You sing it?'

'Ach, I'm not so much a singer, Jack, but I've played it on my pipes often enough. This is my favourite verse: Attomriug indiu neurt nime, soillsi gréine, etrochta ésci, áne thened, déne lóchet, luathi gaithi, fudomna mara, tairismigi talman, cobsaidi alech.'

'Good God, that sounds so old! What does it mean?'

'It means this: 'I bind to myself today the power of heaven, the light of the sun, the whiteness of snow, the force of fire, the flashing of lightning, the speed of wind, the depth of the sea, the stability of the earth, the hardness of the rocks."

Conn ends his recitation, looks at Jack and laughs again.

'I reckon it goes back a long way before the church ever came to Ireland. The old ways, the old beliefs, they endure, even if they're changed to suit the latest face of faith. It's like the pilgrimage itself ...Och, but I'll be boring you, lad.'

'Nae, not at all. Go on, please.'

As their way begins to drop down out of the hills, and they see just the glimmer of the sea in the distance, Conn explains his idea that there's something in human nature that calls people to go travelling, often making actual journeys, perhaps to ancient holy places and shrines as the pilgrims of many faiths do, or perhaps to discover new lands or new seas. Either way, they're going from the known into the unknown. Often the journey involves hardship, difficulty, and danger. But sometimes, Conn says, the most important part of the travelling is done in the mind, and that might be during a physical journey or simply sitting in a chair at home.

'I'm not sure what you mean,' Jack says, puzzled, 'by a journey in the mind?'

'Perhaps I'm not using quite the right word,' Conn replies. 'It's not so much a mental journey in the sense of an imaginary one that I'm meaning. I reckon it's more a journey of the heart or the soul, going inside your self to find what matters, to find a sense of purpose, mebbe to find the divine? I did a lot of travelling in a lot of different lands before I came back to Sara, and I reckon it was all a kind of pilgrimage, but not as some would understand it.' He pauses, musing, then looks across at Jack. 'Did you know the word 'pilgrim' just means someone from beyond, you know, a stranger, a foreigner? Aye, I reckon all of us are from what someone else thinks of as "beyond"!'

CHAPTER FOURTEEN

Lost in their own thoughts, the two men have soon passed the church at Sigrás, crossed over the Rio Mero on the old Roman bridge at O Burgo, and reached the tide mill at Acea da Ma. The miller in Jack is naturally interested in this and rather regrets that MacMorran's mill is too far inland to benefit from the tides at the mouth of the Water of Leith. Powered by the tide, the water supply would be entirely dependable, an advantage over both windmills and other types of watermill.

But then again, Jack thinks, *at least we work regular hours. Tide millers must of course have to work according to the tides – and that means you'd get the power twice a day. Hmm. Might mention it to Miller MacMorran 'though.*

Jack fails consciously to realise that he's assuming he'll go back to his work at the mill and the bakery, and any further thoughts he might have had are interrupted.

'Not far now, Jack,' Conn tells him. 'Mebbe five miles, thereabouts.'

The track is wriggling alongside the banks of the estuary. The tide is out, and it's a bit smelly. There are a few more cottages, but fewer pilgrims – those arriving at A Coruña that morning, coming mainly from Ireland and Wales, have long since passed through.

'Shall we stop here, have a bite to eat?'

'Yes, let's!'

It doesn't take long to wolf down the bread, cold meat, and oranges, and the flagon of watered wine that Sara has packed for them.

'It's all right,' Conn reassures Jack as they remount. 'I'm hoping we can stay at El Valentin tonight. Our friends run it, and they always lay on a good spread for supper!'

El Valentin, Jack discovers when they reach the little port town, is a tavern in a small plaza by the church of San Nicolás. Not far from the harbour, and with two dormitories and three private guest rooms, Conn's friends are kept busy hosting pilgrims and other travellers as they come to and go from A Coruña. They provide three meals a day, which is unusual and very popular. There are tables and benches outside, and from the little first floor balconies, plants trail down their long green stems, the leaves softening the stone exterior and adding a musky scent to the air. As Conn and Jack arrive, the square itself is quiet. Midday is long past, and all right-minded people are enjoying their siesta. Conn goes round to the stables at the back, Jack following. They disturb a lad half asleep on a stack of hay.

'Hola Mateo! Cuida de los caballos hasta mañana por favor.'

Conn slips Mateo a couple of coins, knowing from previous visits that the horses will be well looked after.

'Sí, señor Conn, I look after horses for you. ¿Se queda aquí esta noche? You stay night here?'

'Sí, yes, eso espero!'

Reassured by Mateo that the hostel isn't full, Conn leads the way back to the main door.

'Lorenzo, Bella, hola!' he calls out.

A short, rather stout woman dressed in black bustles through into the bar area. Her face breaks into a beaming smile as she sees who it is.

'Conn! Good to see you, amigo!' She gives Conn a big hug. 'And who this with you?'

'Bella, este es Jack Balfour de Escocia, from Scotland. We've come to find his friend. We think he may be at the Escuela de Muchachos del Mar. Young Mateo said you might have room for us to stay the night?'

'¡Por supuesto! Of course! We have good room for you. And the escuela, it is by el puerto, the port. It is not far. Ah, and here is Lorenzo ...' she says, as her husband emerges from the kitchen, wiping his hands on a cloth.

'Conn, hola! – and Jack, did I hear you say?' Lorenzo shakes their hands. 'And you're staying tonight? Excellent! You speak about el escuela de muchachos del mar, the mariner's school?'

Conn and Jack once again explain their quest to find Robin. Lorenzo easily follows their story. Like his wife, he has a good command of several languages, picked up from their many guests over the years.

'Your friend, this Robin, he is English?'

'No. Half and half, French and Scottish. He was with Soubise, you know, the Huguenot leader? Then he took it into his head to be a mariner and I was told he came here'

Lorenzo is concerned, and shakes his head doubtfully.

'You want I come with you? I know someone there. I can ask him for your friend?'

The three men make their way along the narrow streets and cross a large square, which Lorenzo tells them is the Plaza de María Pita – 'She is heroína against the English!' – and then go through a labyrinth of alleyways. Finally they emerge into the glaring sunshine next to the harbour. The quayside curves round a bay, a long sea wall protecting it from the worst of the weather and the tides.

'Why, if it wasn't for the sunshine,' Jack says, delighted, 'we could be in Leith!'

Indeed, the wharves here are as busy as those Jack is so familiar with. Fishermen are making ready to go out at dusk, trading vessels are being unloaded, carters are heaving goods onto their wagons, merchants and mariners are clogging the lane as they bargain and haggle, and passengers are boarding for their journeys to France, Cornwall, and Ireland. The heady mixture of smells is just like home, as are the sounds, the creak of the boats, the chink of the running rigging, the screams of hungry gulls. And just on the headland, the Escuela de Muchachos del Mar, established by King Felipe just five years ago, gleams in the bright light bouncing off the water.

'What a fine harbour!' Jack says. 'I'm beginning to envy Robin, coming here to learn how to master all these ships!'

'Aye. Sara always says there's something special about sea air, that it clears your mind and lifts your mood … and I reckon she may be right, 'though for me, mountain tops do it too!'

Conn and Jack are smiling, but Lorenzo's face is serious.

Uh-oh, Conn thinks, knowing his friend well. *Lorenzo is looking worried, and that's not good.*

'You wait here,' Lorenzo says, as they approach the gatehouse and the steps leading up to the arched entrance of the school. 'I go ask about the friend. Robin, yes?'

'Robin Logan,' Jack replies, 'from Surgères – but they may think he's English, I don't know?'

'Robin Lo-gan. I ask. Te veo pronto espero – I see you soon,' Lorenzo says, as he walks up the steps and disappears under the arch.

'Thanks!' Jack calls, blithely optimistic that Lorenzo will soon be back, either with his friend or at least with news of him.

While they wait for Lorenzo to return, Conn and Jack mooch along a promontory that leads towards a fort.

'Did you know,' Conn asks, 'that A Coruña was once invaded by Francis Drake? No? That's what Lorenzo was talking about, when we were in the big square, about that heroine of theirs. It was after Drake defeated the armada of ships that King Felipe – the present king's father – sent to invade England. I'm talking nigh on forty years ago, mind. After the battle, the Spanish ships that were left couldn't pass through the Narrow Sea, so they tried to get home round the north of Scotland – and they were all destroyed by storms. Called it the Protestant Wind, Felipe did!'

Rationalist Conn laughs at the bizarre and superstitious thought that the wind, or even God, might be on one side rather than another.

'Spain had been such a mighty power for so long, it must've shaken them. Aye, and it was about then,' he goes on, 'that they began to look more to their own defences. That's when they built this Fort of San Antón. Clever they were, making it star shaped, d'you see? And it's got sloping walls against any artillery fire.' He pauses for a moment, as they both assess and admire the practicality of the little fort.

'That's surely all over now, isn't it? All the warring I mean between England and Spain, and Spain and the Dutch, and, och, I'm not sure who else!' Jack says.

'Ach, you'd have thought so,' Conn replies, 'but we've not long since heard from some of our guests that there's trouble in Bohemia and the Palatinate now. They say the Netherlands and the Spanish are involved again – and even the Danes have been drawn into it too. It's all the same squabble, Catholic against Protestant.'

If Conn were a spitting man, he'd spit with disgust. Instead, he and Jack turn their backs on the fort and head back along the water front. Jack's sharp eyes pick out the figure of Lorenzo, standing at the foot of the steps where they last saw him. He waves.

'There's Lorenzo, see, by the gate-house ... Ach, dammit, but he's on his own.' Jack's face drops ... and then brightens again. 'But of course. Robin couldn't just be let off whatever he's doing, because someone's come to see him. Why, he might be out at sea or anywhere! Och, Jeanne'll be so happy ... and I can get on with, well, with everything else.'

Jack strides out eagerly.

'Lorenzo! What news? Where's Robin?'

Lorenzo's face is glum. He shakes his head.

'Jack, Conn, lo siento, I am so sorry. It is bad news.'

'What! Why? Won't they let him see us?' Jack has it firmly in his mind that Robin is possibly just yards away.

'No, eso no, it is not that. Ach,' Lorenzo sighs, sounding almost Scottish. 'Robin is not here. He ...'

'Not here? You mean, he is at sea? That's what I thought. He'll be training on some ship, or ...'

Conn puts his hand on Jack's arm, silencing him from his increasingly desperate gabble.

'Robin is not here at all. He is not at the escuela. My friend Pepe, he say they laugh at him when he arrive. Pepe say your friend not Spanish, not Catholic, and he has no partidario, um, no supporter, patron. And,' Lorenzo continues with emphasis, 'he admit his experience is only at Battle of Blavet – with los hugonotes. Aie, it can not be worse. I am sorry. He never got further than la entrada. They sent him away.'

'Robin has gone? He was never here, at the school?'

Jack is aghast. He'd dismissed Gaston's concern – and Master Flint's prediction – as mere pessimism, and never seriously considered the possibility that Robin wouldn't be here at the school. Lorenzo shrugs. He's told them the facts. What else can he do?

'Lorenzo,' Conn asks his friend, 'I don't suppose Pepe had any idea what Robin did, where he went, when they turned him away?'

Lorenzo shakes his head. 'No, lo siento, sorry.'

What Lorenzo doesn't tell Conn and Jack is the ridicule and scorn with which the young Robin was regarded by the men and boys at the Escuela. It's a story they'll be laughing over for some time, how a French Huguenot lad turned up, speaking almost no Spanish but all keen and eager and expecting to be accepted. He's either a fool or a madman in their eyes, so why would they care what happened to him, where he went next, let alone think to ask?

It's a doleful trio who make their way back to el Valentin and sit rather heavily down at one of the tables. Bella, preoccupied with supervising the two serving girls, has little time for sympathy. Why this lad didn't just lie about where he'd come from, what his background was, she can't imagine. Ah, the blind confidence of youth!

'What are we to do? Where can Robin have gone?' Jack wonders out loud, his tone shifting between plaintive and petulant. 'I've spent all this time to get here, left the Eagle and everything, and now the damn lad's not even here!'

Not much gets past Bella's two maid-servants. They've been eyeing Jack and now go into a huddle, whispering together. Not much gets past Bella either.

'¡Oiga, ustedes dos! ¿De qué estás susurrando? What you whisper?' she asks them.

The taller girl replies, using her limited English to impress Jack.

'Señora, the young man,' she blushes as she glances at him, 'he is looking for friend?'

Jack's ears prick up.

'Do you know something, señorita? My friend Robin went to join the school and was turned away. I need to find him.'

More whispering, then the girl speaks again.

'Sí, señor. My sister …' she indicates the other girl '… she work sometime at other place, hostel for peregrinos, pil-grim? She say is boy work there two, per'aps three week. He is boy who cannot join escuela. He is not Español, he is Hugonote. It is good for him at hostel – many people come, go, peregrinos, viajeros – um, walking people? At hostel is none care where from, just do work, be agreeable …'

After another exchange with her sister, the girl continues, 'Juanita, she say she is not there since two, three day, but he is there then.'

Jack releases the breath he's been hardly aware of holding, leaps to his feet, and causes much blushing and laughter when he gives each of the maids a kiss on the cheek.

'Gracias, señoritas! This is such good news! So Robin is working at a hostel, yes? Will you take me there now? Will he be there?'

It is agreed. Juanita will take Jack to the hostel to find Robin. Conn will stay at el Valentin and give Lorenzo and Bella a hand if they get busy before Juanita gets back. As Jack is led through yet another maze of little alleys, his despondancy is a thing of the past. *Thank God Robin's done something sensible at last,* he thinks, *and not gone haring off somewhere else! I daresay he'll have needed to earn money to get home again after the huge embarrassment of being rejected at the school. Och, and he'll be happy to know Jeanne and I've come to fetch him back.*

Hostal Alboran is on the outskirts of the little town, in a poorer area than el Valentin. It's conveniently situated on the route that the pilgrims would take as they head for Santiago de Compostela – or back again to board their ship and sail for home after their pilgrimage is completed. It's a bit shabby, but Jack doesn't even notice, let alone care. He follows Juanita inside. After the glare of the sun, it seems dark, and he takes a moment to get his bearings. They're in a narrow lobby area. Opposite the main entrance that they've just come through, another door, currently wide open, leads out into a courtyard. There are people everywhere, talking and laughing, rubbing their sore feet, stretching their well-walked legs, collecting their clothes from the drying line, stuffing things into their packs. They all seem happy, if a bit tired and a bit dirty.

'Go home,' Juanita startles Jack.

'What?'

She points randomly at the guests. 'Peregrinaje es final, end. To-morrow on boat. Go home.'

'Oh, yes,' he laughs. 'I thought you meant me! These people are all on their way home?'

'Sí' Juanita is pleased that he now understands, and gives him a beaming smile, flicking her long dark hair off her shoulder … 'After, before dark, boat arrive, new peregrinos. Here tonight, to-morrow um …' Forgetting the word for 'walk' Juanita uses her fingers to show what she means.

'Ah, more walkers arrive later and set off tomorrow. I've got it. And Robin, my friend? Do you know where he will be?'

'In day, clean. Now, food … cochinando. Come.'

She leads Jack confidently through another door, away from the hubbub of the hall and the courtyard. A smell of food wafts towards them and Jack sniffs appreciatively, although he's privately smiling at the thought of young Robin let loose in a kitchen. Unless he's learnt a lot recently, Jack hopes the pilgrims have strong stomachs. Juanita is now deep in conversation with an older man and woman – perhaps the proprietors? They have that air about them. She turns and points at Jack, then launches off again in Spanish too rapid to follow. Arms are waving, voices are rising, and Juanita is not looking happy. Eventually she turns, flushed and frowning.

'Juanita? What is it? Where's Robin?'

'Oof!' She lets out a big sigh. 'I am say to Salvador and Pilar, you come to take Robin home. They say no, no go home, is good obrero … work man? Good clean, good in cocina, kit-chen.'

'Oh!' Jack is dumb-founded.

These people don't want Robin to leave? He's a good worker?

'But is Robin here?' he asks.

Apparently not, but Jack is relieved to be told that he'll be back soon. He's gone to meet the boat that's expected any minute now. Because he's a native English speaker, he's likely to collect a good number of pilgrims and bring them back to stay at the hostel overnight.

'You wait? Wait for friend?'

'Yes, um, sí, gracias.'

Juanita reluctantly leaves Jack and heads back to work at el Valentin. Salvador and Pilar, having pressed a cup of wine into Jack's hand, also excuse themselves.

'Per favor, wait in courtyard? Rob-in here pronto.'

Settling himself on a bench, Jack idly watches the guests coming and going, listens to the splash of a tiny fountain set in the centre, sips his wine. After a few minutes he's joined by a couple of young men, who, having cleaned themselves up after the day's walk, are waiting for their supper to be served.

'Buenas noches!' one of them greets Jack, in such a strange accent that he instantly knows this is not a Spaniard.

''Evening,' he replies. 'Have you had a good walk today?'

The two men, Ciarán and Petroc, have indeed had a good walk, all the way from O Mesón do Vento, about six hours, and mostly downhill.

'We'll be off on the ship first thing tomorrow – and I hope it's not as rough as it was coming!' one of them says. 'Ugh! Give me solid land any day!'

'Ah, but it's been worth it,' the other one chips in. 'I've wanted to do this all my life, and now I have! I've walked the Way, and seen the saint's bones at Compostela!'

The two friends are full of enthusiasm. They tell Jack how they walked from Marazion –

'Near Penzance, where the wee island is, Karrek Loos yn Koos. What? You don't know it? You've not been to Cornwall? By God, lad, you've not lived!'

– to Plymouth, to catch their ship, bound for A Coruña. They describe the increasingly powerful pull they felt as they got closer to Santiago, how emotional and humbling it was finally to arrive at the shrine and to attend the mass. They reflect on how they'll take home with them many precious memories, not just of their arrival, but of the land itself and the people they've met along the way. In a corner of his mind, Jack rather regrets his scepticism about such things as shrines, holy bones, indulgences – generally, the whole concept of pilgrimage, despite the re-interpretation that Conn had shared with him earlier.

'We had it easy really,' Petroc says. 'Once we'd landed here, we only had to walk two days there, then a rest day in the town, and two days back. Some people walk for weeks, months even just to get there, never mind getting home again. That takes some strength of mind as well as body, you know.'

'Aye,' Jack replies. 'I do know! I've walked here from Bilbao. Well,' honesty compels him to add, 'I rode from Carral ... but I walked the rest.'

'God bless you, mate! And will you not go that bit further, to Santiago? It seems a shame not to, now you've come so far? You may never come this way again.'

Jack shakes his head. 'I don't think so. I'm here to find my friend.'

As Jack speaks, the main door opens wide and a group of people bursts in. Ciarán and Petroc move out of the way – 'See you later mebbe!' – and Salvador and Pilar come out to greet the newcomers, directing them towards the dormitories, the washrooms, and the dining hall. At last Jack sees the person he's looking for, ushering the stragglers in and closing the door behind them.

'Robin! Robin, over here! It's me, Jack!'

Robin's jaw drops in amazement.

'Jack? Jack Balfour? What in heaven's name are you doing here! Just wait one moment. Don't go away!'

As if I would, after all the trouble I've taken to find you, Jack thinks.

Robin, looking tanned, fit, and happy, is speaking to Pilar – and sounding, to Jack's ears, surprisingly fluent in Spanish.

'Señora Pilar, los quince por una noche. Dinero con alimento, está bien? Um ... y mi amigo aqui. Hablo con él ahora?'

Whatever Robin is saying seems to be approved of. Pilar smiles, pats his arm, and nods.

'Unos minutos, luego debemos servir la comida' she says, before disappearing back into the kitchen area, leaving Salvador still shepherding the new arrivals.

Robin wends his way through them back to Jack. He claps him on the shoulder.

'I've got a few minutes, but then I must help serve the meal. It's all go, Jack! But tell me, what in God's name are you doing here?'

'I've come for you, Robin. I've come to fetch you home.'

'What?' Robin looks even more incredulous than before. 'Sorry, Jack. It's great to see you, but you may have had a wasted journey. I've no intention of going home.'

CHAPTER FIFTEEN

'Robin, don't be jesting with me now – I've come a long way to find you! Come on, get your stuff and we'll get back to el Valentin. Conn's waiting for us there. Then tomorrow we'll ...'

'No, sorry, Jack. I'm not jesting. I couldn't be more serious! I'm not going anywhere, tonight or tomorrow or any day soon. I've got work here, I'm earning good money, I'm learning Spanish ...'

Jack slumps down onto one of the benches.

I can't believe this. I've come all this way to get him, and now he says he's not coming home?

But Robin is still speaking.

'I know I made a bit of a fool of myself, turning up at the escuela – did you hear about that? Ah, yes, I see you did! Aye, it was a bit embarrassing. But I've learnt from that. And I've met this chap Miguel ...'

'Robin! ¡Rápidamente!'

'Ach, bugger! ¡Ya voy, Pilar!' he calls. 'Sorry, Jack. That's Pilar calling me. I must get back to work. Listen, did you mention el Valentin? That's where you're staying?'

'Aye, it is.'

'I'll come over when I've finished here. I can tell you my plans, all right?'

Three hours later, Jack, Robin, and Conn, gathered around a table at el Valentin, seem to have reached a deadlock. Lorenzo has re-filled the jug of local wine and removed the trenchers after Bella's roast lamb was wolfed down, but now, sensing tension in the air, he's staying at a safe distance. Robin, so full of his plans, so eager to share them when he arrived, and so shocked to learn that Jeanne was the instigator of the search for him –

What? She's waiting for me at Carral! I don't believe it! Why would she do that? She'll spoil everything!

– is leaning back in his chair, arms crossed on his chest. Conn has one elbow on the table, his hand cupping his chin as he listens to all that's said, biding his time, but Jack hardly knows whether he's feeling more furious or more envious or more stupid, as he realises his self-adopted role of hero-saviour couldn't be less appropriate.

Robin has it all sorted out, he thinks, his lips twisting in a slight scowl.

'Jack, don't look at me like that, mate!' Robin says. 'This is the chance I've been waiting for all my life. You can't blame me that my parents never got my letter telling them all about it, nor that Pa's broken his leg! Och, but it's great to know Gaston and the others valued what I did in the battle. He's right, Gaston is … you know, what he said to you about how I love the sea – I do! And he's right that I'm not cut out to be a soldier.' Robin shakes his head. 'No, fighting's not for me. If it was, I'd have stayed with them on the Île de Ré. But I do want to sail, Jack, and you know yourself what that longing's like. Why, that's how come you're here, isn't it – having your wee adventure on the Eagle! And …'

'Aye, I know, Robin,' Jack breaks in, 'and you're right. For me, it is just a 'wee adventure'. I'll soon be going back – back to the mill, back to the bakery, back to Jennie, if she'll have me …'

Jennie? Who's Jennie? Robin wonders, but wisely says nothing, while Conn gives him a nod and the glimmer of a smile.

'… but you – well, you don't know how long this escapade will last, do you? What about your parents' estate? Who's going to look after that? Monsieur Morel can't do it all on his own. And what about Jeanne? How's she going to feel when I tell her that her fiancé's run away to sea?'

At this, Robin sits upright. Jack's interference may be well-meaning, but he's had just about enough.

'Ach, working the estate's not for me, Jack. It never was. Jon's best suited to that, and we all know it. It'd really put his nose out of joint – and old Morel's – if I decided to try my hand at running the place! And like I told you, Jeanne may call herself my fiancée, and yes, we probably will marry, but that won't be for years yet. I'm only sixteen, for God's sake!'

Jack has run out of arguments, but Conn has yet to have his say.

'Robin, we hear what you say. I daresay you can understand why we're a bit taken aback … but for what it's worth, I reckon you're doing well. You've found out that fighting's not for you but that seafaring is. You've picked yourself up after that fiasco at the school here. You've got yourself work, you're learning the language, and you've made some contacts, yes?'

'Yes!' Robin's face brightens at this praise and he sits forward, elbows on the table. 'You may not have heard – and it may mean nothing to you – but word came a week or so ago that the Admiral's regained São Salvador da Bahia from the Dutch, and so …'

'Hang on! Who's regained what?'

'Oh, the Admiral, Fadrique de Toledo. You must have heard of him! No? Well, he's only the General of Portugal, and the Capitán General of the Navy, as well as leading the army of Brazil. But the point is, he's got São Salvador back from the Dutch.'

'Well, good for him!' Jack says, rather grumpily, raising his glass as if in a toast, and taking another mouthful of wine. 'But how does that affect you?'

Oh God, I'm not sure I really want to know the answer to that! Jack realises, the moment the words are out of his mouth. *Did he say Brazil?*

'Sorry, I'm not explaining very well. Now that we've got São Salvador back …'

'*We*', thinks Jack, *who's this 'we'? First, he adopts the Huguenots, now he adopts the Spanish?*

'… it means that the trade can start up again, you know, in sugarcane? That's just as important as the Flota de Indias, the Treasure Fleet, you know, for all it brings silver and gold! I've been hanging around the harbour a bit. Since I've learnt some

Spanish I can pick things up, and Miguel says there's a boat bound for Cádiz that leaves next week. We plan to be on it. He says that's the best place to go, to be picked for crew.'

Robin takes a swig of his wine, looking triumphant. Jack is little the wiser.

'I'm not sure I'm getting your meaning, Robin. This Admiral's re-taken a place in Brazil, so now trading in sugarcane can get going again, yes?'

Robin nods, a little impatiently.

Isn't it obvious? God save us, but Jack's being awfully slow! I don't remember him being so dim ... but then, he is just a baker from Restalrig. Can anything good come from there?

'And you're planning to go with this friend to Cadiz, wherever that is ... no, don't tell me now,' Jack continues. 'And Cadiz is the place to be picked for crew ... but crew for what?'

'For the merchant ships, of course, the traders going to the Americas, to Brazil. Miguel isn't much older than me, but he's worked as crew for years. He says they don't just bring the sugar back here, they take it to the Carib Islands and to New England. There's so much opportunity, Jack, and ...'

Robin stops in mid-sentence. Conn is narrowing his eyes, shaking his head almost imperceptibly.

Oh, I've said enough? And I was just getting into it!

Silence falls for a few moments. All the other guests have long since left the bar, and the tables inside and out have been cleared and cleaned. A few stragglers can be heard in the street making their way home. Across the square, the church bell tolls eleven. Finally, Jack stirs, scratches his head, looks directly at his old friend.

'Ach, Robin, what can I say? All those weeks walking here from Bilbao, I never imagined anything like this. To be honest, earlier on, when I was waiting for you at the hostel, I thought you'd be feeling sorry for yourself, after being turned away from the school and everything ...'

Jack pauses, as Robin shrugs and looks unconcerned.

That was weeks ago! Who cares about that now?

'... but I was wrong. Here you are, all fired up and setting sail for the New World, by God – and you don't need rescuing at all!'

And how embarrassing that I got it so wrong! Jack thinks as he speaks. He laughs.

'It's my own fault. I should've known you better! You were always one to find your own way. And if I'm honest,' Jack admits, 'I can't say it doesn't sound marvellous. Why, I've half a mind to come with you and your new friend – Miguel was it? No ...' he hastily stops Robin's enthusiastic response, '... absolutely not! I've other things to do. But Robin, what about Jeanne? What do I tell her?'

'Tell her the truth ...' Robin begins to say, but Conn is wiser.

'No, Robin. It's not fair to expect Jack to do your dirty work for you. He and Jeanne have come a long way out of love and concern for you. They may have been misguided about your needs, but they did it. The least you can do is tell the lass yourself, face to face, just what your plans are. And if they do include her in the future, then you need to tell her that too. Have a heart, lad. It's not all about you!'

Eleven miles away, Jeanne is also sitting at a table, enjoying a last mug of herbal tea with Sara after their busy day. The fire is dying down, the candles offering a gentle light. Outside owls can be heard hooting over the constant splash of the stream.

'I am like to have the company of another woman,' Sara says, 'and you are such a help for me, to be doing out the rooms, so I have the time in el jardín and the still room. Oh, and please do not let me be forgetting again to take el loción to Vera mañana, yes? I am promise her some. I make it from wolfsbane, grosellas, and romero – you would be saying rosmarin, rose-mary? It is very good, making strong the músculos in the legs and arms. They are being tired for Vera from the making of the hogazas de pan ... um ... the bread, le pain?'

Jeanne smiles.

'I'll try to remind you. Jacques tells me it is hard work, the pétrissage, kneading. And I am happy to help you. At home, I am help with Jesette – Robin's maman – but she has a house-keeper and maid, so it is not so much to do.'

'Ah, sí. You are living with la familia da Robin? Not with your own familia?'

'I am not have any famille,' Jeanne explains. 'I am bébé when mes parents, they are die from la rugeole, um … fever with red spots? I do not remember them. There is no other famille left, all are dead. Mon père, he is work for l'Ambassadeur Cosse. When he and ma mère die, it is the same year Jesette – his daughter, you know? – is marrying Rab. So Grandpère Cosse – this is what I call him – he and Grandmère Madeleine, they are taking me in and I am living with them. It is very comfortable, very easy. They are good to me. When Grandpère die, Grandmère Madeleine, she is gone to live avec sa sœur, her sister. Then Rab and Jesette and Robin and Jon, they are come from Écosse, Scotland, to live in Surgères. Before, they visit many time, so I am knowing them all. Robin and I, we are promise to marry since we are enfants. Oh, Sara,' Jeanne hesitates, anxiety pleating her forehead, 'I hope I am doing right, coming here, to find my Robin. It is just I am afraid for him. But he may not be happy that I come … And my hair! What will he think of me?'

Dios mío, Sara thinks. *¡Es un poco tarde ahora – a little late now!*

'I understand,' she says instead, patting Jeanne's arm sympa-thetically. 'It's natural to worry. My sister is the same, long time ago when we follow Hendrie – Jacobo's padre you know? – to Escocia. All is be well, Jeanne, do not be worry. And if not well, then some other, some better, will be. Yes!' Sara insists, smil-ing at Jeanne's sceptical expression. 'I am believe it. But now is time for sleep, and mañana we are muy ocupadas, so before we are know it, Conn and Jacobo and your Rob-in, they will come.'

Sara is right. She and Jeanne have a busy morning. They water the garden before the sun is up, check the bee-hives, give the guests their breakfasts and see them on their way, and then clean and change the rooms. Once all the chores are done, the two women take the short walk to the market square, to give Vera her lotion and get fresh bread. There's no time for Jeanne to fret. They're just leaving Vera's bakery when they hear the sound of hooves, clip-clopping towards them. Turning, they see a figure sliding off the saddle he's been sharing with Jack, and come running towards them.

'Jeanne! Jeanne!'

'Robin!'

Turning their smiling faces away from the youngsters' passionate reunion, Conn, Sara, and Jack make their way back to el Hogar. By the time they get there, Sara has been brought up to date with the essentials.

'So Rob-in is not go home, he is go to sea?'

'Yes, mo chara,' Conn says, giving his wife a wry smile. 'Who does that remind you of, eh?'

As they laugh, Jack, having no idea what the jest is, takes the armful of loaves through to the kitchen. Sara soon joins him and busies herself getting the dinner ready. Conn, having seen to the horses, comes in through the scullery.

'That smells good! Are we waiting for Jeanne and Robin, or can we start without them?'

'Ah, I think we'd be waiting a while,' Sara replies.

In fact Robin and Jeanne join them quite soon, Jeanne flushed and giggling, Robin looking smug. The kitchen table at dinner-time is, as ever, the place for conversation, for news, for announcements, and for debate.

'Rob-in, it is good to meet you!' Sara welcomes the young man with a hug. 'Come, sit and eat. I'll fetch ... oh, Jeanne, thank you, you are already do it.'

Almost welded to Robin's side, Jeanne looks happier than Jack has ever seen her.

'So Jeanne,' he dives in, 'has young Robin told you his plans?'

'Oh yes, Jacques.' She dimples up at Robin. 'He is going to be merchant to the Americas! It is so exciting, I ...'

'Well, just a crew member first, if they'll have me,' Robin interrupts, with unusual modesty, 'but mebbe one day I'll have my own ship, and ...'

'But first, before he go next week to Cadiz,' Jeanne interrupts eagerly, the words tumbling from her mouth, 'we go together to Santiago, to finish le pèlerinage I am begin with Jacques! Robin is not go back to work à l'auberge ...'

'Aye, Salvador and Pilar were vexed when I asked for a few days off, said not to bother going back. Pity ... but it means we can go to Santiago. Everyone at the hostel talks about nothing else!'

'We walk two days, see the saint, stay one night, walk back. Then Robin, he is go with Miguel, and I ... '

Jeanne's voice, high and shrill with excitement, suddenly tails off, and her flushed face pales.

Oh, et puis quoi? Then what will I do?

Sara gives a questioning glance to Conn who nods. Sometimes there is no need for words.

'And you,' Sara says, 'per'aps you are staying here at el Hogar with me? Conn is often going with los peregrinos, as un guía, a guide. I would like it, to have you here, if tu familia are not saying no.'

'Oh! Oh oui! Oui, j'aimerais rester ici ... I would love to stay here. I will be no trouble, I promise!'

She dashes around the table, gives Sara kisses on both cheeks, and receives a hug from Conn before plonking herself down – 'Oof! You great lump!' – on Robin's lap, twining her arms around his neck.

What a show! Jack thinks. *And I suppose I'm the numbskull who has to tell Rab and Jesette and Jon all this?*

Conn has noticed Jack's resigned expression and gives him a wink.

He's a good lad, he thinks. *Why should he let himself be taken for granted?*

'So now you two have decided what you're doing,' he says, 'who's going to tell Rab and Jesette and Jon? It's not fair to expect Jack to go all the way back there, is it?'

In fact Conn already has the solution to the question he's posed, but he enjoys stirring the young couple's consciences. Sara bites her lips together to stop her laughter bubbling out at her husband's mischief.

God, I like this man! Jack thinks.

'Oh, erm … yes, I mean no. Of course I wouldn't expect Jack …' Robin blusters, thinking *Bugger! Conn's not wrong. I had assumed Jack would tell them. Damn and blast!*

Jeanne's mind has simply gone blank.

Conn lets the confusion hang in the air for a few more moments.

'Sara, I wonder, can you think of a solution?' he asks, with a glint in his eye.

Rolling her eyes at him, joining the game, Sara says, 'Hm … I wonder … I am think of the son of Lorenzo and Bella …'

'Ah, Sara, of course!' Conn says, grinning, as if this was a new idea. 'Yes, their elder son Lucas – guess what? He's a merchant, would you believe, between Cadiz, A Coruña, and Bordeaux … Aye,' he responds to Robin's gush of exclamations and questions, 'it might well be one of his ships you'll be on next week – and perhaps stay on after that. So when you go back to A Coruña, after your pilgrimage, how about you have a word with Lorenzo, perhaps meet Lucas? With the right incentive,' Conn rubs his thumb and fingers together, 'it shouldn't be too hard for him to take a message for you to Bordeaux – and even on to Surgères, and …'

'But send two copies!' Jack interrupts. 'One to Surgères and one to Marans, just in case, eh?'

CHAPTER SIXTEEN

Despite the usual turnover of guests, El Hogar seems quiet the following day after Robin and Jeanne have set off for Santiago de Compostela, a jar of Sara's special lotion tucked into Robin's pack – 'for the tired legs!' While Sara herself is busy in her garden, Conn finds Jack sitting on the sloping grassy bank, gazing at the little stream that gurgles its way over their land.

'Jack, lad, there you are!' Conn says. 'I'm going to ride over to A Coruña and back today. I want to forewarn my friend Lorenzo and his son Lucas about young Robin's plans and his need for a messenger – and mebbe a berth! But I was wondering, d'you want to come with me? We're not trying to get rid of you,' he adds hastily with a smile, 'but I know your time's limited now, isn't it? So I reckon you'll be looking for a passage as soon as you can?'

'Aye, you're right. Ach, I never thought I'd be saying this, Conn, but I'm looking forward to going home. I was just thinking about it. This time away, well, it's been great, and I wouldn't have missed any of it for the world, even the bad stuff!' He laughs. 'I'll have lots of stories to tell for the rest of my life!'

'I know what you mean, and I felt the same when I was on the road,' Conn agrees. 'But there comes a time, doesn't there, when you're ready ... perhaps not to go back to how things were, because travel changes you, changes your perspective and your priorities ...'

'Exactly! I do want to go back, but not to how it was. Och, if Miller MacMorran will still have me, I'll be glad to go back to working at the mill and the bakery for the time being ... and I know Uncle Will and Aunt Elspeth would happily have me back at Hawkhill with them and David and Harry, but ...'

'Yes? You said, 'for the time being'. Have you something else in mind?'

'Aye, I have, 'though it's all a bit new yet. It's about the Tor, the house where I was born, you know? No one has lived there since Ma died. Pa and Maria got a place in Edinburgh, and we lads were with Ma Mayne for, och, five, six years? Then we went to Hawkhill. But the Tor was never sold. It's just stood empty. And it's mine, actually. Billy inherited Ma's cottage, and the Tor came to me. Uncle Will's kept an eye on it, but I've never given it any thought until now.'

'And you've a mind now to live there yourself, mebbe?' Conn asks gently, aware that the death of Jack's mother, Geillis, is a difficult subject, linked in the family's minds with the discovery of his father's long-standing affaire with Sara's older sister Maria.

'Aye. As I say, I'd never thought of it before. I reckon we all just put the place out of our minds ... And it'll seem odd at first, perhaps, even a bit painful ...'

Jack sounds wistful. His mouth forms a tight line, and for a moment he screws up his eyes as if to prevent deep-seated memories and emotions from escaping. But after a few seconds, he shakes his head slightly and gives a rueful smile.

'Ach, but the past's the past, isn't it, Conn ... and I've a wee plan. It only came to me this morning, when I fetched the bread from Vera's. I'm thinking, perhaps I could make a bakery at the Tor, get the flour from MacMorran, supply the village ...' Jack begins to speak more quickly, as enthusiasm surges through him. 'I've some new ideas, and not just for bread. It's easier to get wheat from the continent now, as well as our own oats and barley, and that means I can make so many more things, different things, that'll make my place stand out.'

He pauses, aware that Conn is patiently listening.

'Sorry, Conn. I didn't mean to go on, when you're wanting to get off to A Coruña.'

'Jack, it sounds like a fine plan. Your ma was a great baker, wasn't she? I remember your Aunt Missy saying so.'

Jack nods. 'Aye, she was. That's how I remember her, at home, with her apron on and her hands all floury, humming as she worked ... I think mebbe I've inherited it from her, like Billy inherited his love of horses from our grandpa Cameron. Ma always encouraged me in the kitchen. Baking was what we did together, just her and me, you know?'

'But you'd live there too, wouldn't you? It wouldn't just be a bakery?'

'Aye, that's right, and it'll take a while to get it all done. That's why I'd need to go back to MacMorran's to start with. But mebbe, after that …

Jack drifts off, and Conn can't help but smile, rightly suspecting that the younger man is hoping that a home and a business – added to his good self – might be a fair offer to make for Jennie's hand.

'So, all the more important to get back home then, eh?' he chivvies Jack. 'Can you be ready in ten minutes? I'll get the horses saddled up, while you fetch your pack.'

After an affectionate farewell with Sara, and having given her a rather reluctant promise to visit her sister Maria and his nine-year-old half-brother Robert, Jack is quiet on the ride to A Coruña. Conn wisely doesn't interrupt his reverie. He himself is thinking back some thirteen or fourteen years, to when he was about Jack's age and had gone on his own travels. Wild and good years they were, with lots of hard times, a myriad of new experiences and impressions, some loneliness, and many memories. Conn had never guessed the road would take him to so many places: across Europe – from Bruges to Aachen, Leipzig and Danzig, on to Constantinople and the Holy Land, along the north coast of Africa …

… and finally, finally, Conn remembers now, *between the Pillars of Hercules to Spain – and Sara. Round in a circle and home again … and I never did get to Rome! Ah, but it was enough. If this wee adventure has been enough for young Jack, if he's truly ready to settle down, and if – another if! – Jennie's the right one for him, well, he might just end up being as happy as I am!*

For Jack, this short journey feels like the end of something, the end of his adventure, even the end of his youth. He's turning towards home, towards his future – and he feels a curious and poignant mixture of regret and anticipation that makes his stomach churn.

What if Jennie says no ... or has found someone else ... or has gone to the New World? And what if I can't make a go of it at the Tor? What if Miller MacMorran opposes me?

For a few minutes, Jack's heart is in his boots, and without realising it, he pulls his horse to a halt. Conn doubles back.

'All right, Jack?'

'Ach, just, you know ...'

'Aye, I reckon I do. Just do the best you can, lad. You can't anticipate everything! I've heard some say that what's for you won't pass you by, but that sounds like we've no choice in the matter. You know I crewed on some ships like you did, yes? When I felt unsure, and all the ifs and buts were getting me down, I used to picture what the captain did: he steered a course, adjusted it according to the wind, the weather, the rocks – aye, and the wrecks in your case! Steer and adjust, steer and adjust ... and in the end, he brings his ship into port. I like to think that that's what we have to do – steer and adjust ... and then adjust again. All right?'

'Aye, that makes sense. Thanks, Conn. Thanks for everything.'

Reaching A Coruña, Conn and Jack once again head for el Valentin, where Conn brings Lorenzo up to date with Robin's plans and his need for a messenger to Surgères.

'Por supuesto! Of course! Lucas can help with this. He has two ships leaving next week, one for Bordeaux and one for Cadiz. It could not be mas perfecto, more perfect, for your young friend, sí? Un barco por mensaje, un barco para él! And Robin has un amigo with him? No hay problema. I speak to Lucas. He will be happy of more crew. But Jacobo, you are not going with Robin and his friend?'

'No. I need to go home, to Scotland, Escocia. Do you know, is there a ship, un barco?'

'I think ... what day is it? Sí, mañana, or the day after, I am not sure. You stay tonight here?'

Having secured his bed for the night, Jack is anxious to ensure his passage home.

'Lorenzo, I'll be back later, for supper. I need to check on the ships. Conn, will you still be here?'

'No, my lad. I want to get back to Sara,' Conn replies, giving Jack a bear-hug that reminds him of his Uncle Will. 'Travel safely, Jack. And when you can, let us know … well, how things work out, all right?'

Jack swallows down the lump in his throat as Conn swings himself back up into the saddle of his horse, takes the reins of the other, and turns back the way they came. Just a brief wave – 'Adios, mi amigo! God go with you!' – and he's gone.

Halfway to the harbour, Jack realises he's still got his pack on his back.

Ach, that was stupid, I should've left it with Lorenzo! Goodness, but I feel just the same as I did leaving Will at Leith – except there's no Sam waving to me this time. Ah, but there's the quayside – and a good number of ships in dock.

The harbourmaster tells Jack he has a choice of ships for his passage back. The Cervellione will leave tomorrow, calling first at Bordeaux and then Vannes, before crossing to Ireland and the west coast of Scotland. Her sister ship, Orosia, leaving the following day, will go straight to Brest, then London, Lynn, and Leith. Jack chooses the latter, Orosia. Being told she already has a full complement of crew, he pays for his passage from the little purse of money that Conn and Sara insisted he take, knowing his own precious savings had been stolen. When he had tried to refuse, Sara said:

'You are like family for me, Jacobo. We are not having our own small ones, but you are como mi sobrino, like nephew. So please, let us help. Then one day, you will help another like this, yes?'

Now, as he thankfully tucks the receipt safely away down his boot leg, Jack thinks, *So that's that. Two nights here, and then home. It's nearly over.*

Loathe to leave the hustle and bustle of the busy harbour, the screech of the gulls, the smell of fish, and the salty air, Jack squats against a wall, rifling through his pack. He pulls out his flageolet – *I'll finally have time to try to mend this while I'm on board* – and the lace for his aunt, which Sara has washed and pressed, so it looks as good as new.

But where's Rab's book? Ah, down at the bottom, of course. I've still a fair bit to read, now I've got the pages back in order.

The book is looking rather the worse for wear, after being torn apart and reassembled, but Jack's keen to get to the end of Galileo's treatise. He settles himself on a bitt, knowing the sun and his stomach will together tell him when it's time to go back to el Valentin for supper, and is soon absorbed.

'¡Ese es el! Ese es el chico que intentó entrar a la escuela. ¡Sí, el chico hugonote! ¡Atrápalo, rápido!'

Shouting disturbs Jack. Looking up, he sees three, perhaps four, young men, emerging from the mariners' school and running in his direction. Before he knows it, his book is torn out of his hands, he's pulled to his feet, and his arms are grasped tightly.

'What the ...'

'You are spy boy!' one of the men almost spits in Jack's face. 'English spy boy from damn Huguenots! Yes,' he insists against Jack's denials, 'it is you, and now you will answer for what you do!'

CHAPTER SEVENTEEN

'I don't know what you're talking about!' Jack shouts, as his attackers begin to drag him and his pack towards the gatehouse of the school. 'And I'm not English, I'm Scots!'

The youths are not interested in Jack's protests.

'Spy-boy!'

'No! What are you doing? Leave me alone! Stop this!'

Despite his best efforts, Jack can't get free of them. Knots of people are staring, pointing, cat-calling: 'El es el espía!' 'Extranjero!' 'Traidor inglés!'

God's teeth, thinks Jack, *I don't understand! What are they saying?*

'Let me go!'

At the gatehouse of the escuela, an older man is standing, tall, pale, expressionless.

'Tráelo adentro. Bring him inside,' he says, and Jack is dragged through the doorway, dumped on a bench, his book thrown on the floor, his pack upended and shaken out.

'¿Este es el chico de los hugonotes? ¿Estás seguro?'

'¡Sí, es él! No lo vimos, pero Marcos nos habló de él. Debe ser él!'

It's all just a babble to Jack, and a frightening one. The only words he picks out are 'chico' and 'hugonotes'.

Something about the Huguenots? And a boy? And I'm the boy? But I only went there looking for Robin. How could they know that? And why pick on me because of it?

The youths have apparently been dismissed. They reluctantly lope out of the door, regretting that their moment of glory is over and that they weren't allowed to take the spy-boy into a quiet corner and wreak their revenge with fists and boots.

'Soy el maestro de la escuela. Se me ha informado que buscas entrar aquí, y ...'

I've no idea what he's talking about, Jack thinks, as anger overtakes his shock and fear. *And I don't like the way he's towering over me like that.*

He stands up, shakes his head, crosses his slightly shaking arms over his chest.

'Lo siento,' he says in as firm a voice as he can manage. 'No hablo español. I regret, sir, that I don't speak Spanish. Why did those ruffians set on me like that and bring me here? I've done nothing wrong. And who are you anyway?'

'¿No hablas español? Entonces como … If you don't speak Spanish then how did you expect to be accepted here at my school? I have heard how you tried to join, some weeks ago. Now you are here again, yes, come to see the results of your dirty work!'

'You are mistaken,' Jack replies, drawing himself up to his full height, channelling his Uncle Michael, Lord Balfour of Burleigh, former Master of the King's Household and Ambassador to the Duke of Tuscany. 'I have never tried to enter this school,' he says honestly, and speaking with what he hopes will pass as the aristocratic tone of his ancestors. 'Why would I? I am not some common seaman, nor do I wish to be. I am Johne Balfour, son of Captain Sir Hendrie Balfour, grandson of James, Lord Pittendreich. I am a Scotsman … escocés, no inglés.'

'¿Cómo? ¿Escocés? Algo no está bien. Espera aquí. Something not is right. Wait here, um, por favor.'

As the Master leaves the room, Jack sinks down onto the bench again.

What on earth is going on? Have they mistaken me for Robin? And what do they think Robin's done, for goodness sake? But that old maestro, whoever he is, he's not used to being stood up to!'

Jack approaches the door and tries the handle, but of course, it's locked. He peers out of the window. Nothing is happening. People are going about their business again, but fewer of them now, as dusk turns the sky from blue to mauve and the first stars appear. A couple of small boats are setting out for their evening's fishing. A rowdy gang of mariners sway out of an inn, arm in arm, whistling and gesturing at a couple of girls. Abandoning the view, Jack paces to and fro, perches on the bench, paces again. His stomach gives an enormous rumble: it's way past supper time.

How long can they keep me here? Jack wonders, *and why do they want to? I've told them who I am – and it's the truth, for God's sake. What do they mean 'spy-boy'? Even if they do think I'm Robin, they surely know he never even got through the entrance, so what's all the fuss about?*

In the end, Jack sits on the bench again, slumping with his back against the wall, and lapsing into a light doze. It seems like hours later when he's roused by the sound of voices outside, in Spanish of course. Loud and argumentative, there seem to be three or perhaps four speakers, and one of them a woman. He catches odd words: '... chico espía ... hugonotes ... Escocés ...' Jack is alert and at the window in a flash.

They're talking, arguing, about me! Och, it's Lorenzo and Juanita from el Valentin, with one of those ruffians that grabbed me, and some other man ... Och, thank God they've come and found me!

A few minutes later, the door opens.

'Lorenzo! Juanita! I'm here, it's me, Jack! I ...'

'Jacobo, we wait for you here.' Lorenzo sounds calm. 'No worry. Es un error. Este hombre, this man, he explicará, explain you.'

The man comes in, leaving the door ajar. Jack stands, ready to don his invisible cloak of haughtiness again, but it seems it won't be necessary. This man offers Jack a slight bow, and his tone is conciliatory.

'My Lord Balfour,' he begins, and Jack's eyebrows rise, as he suppresses a smirk.

Well, I'm not going to correct him!

'El Maestro send his apologia. He is mal informado. Tus amigos, your people ...' he points back through the door, 'they explicado to him. Los estudiantes, they are too hasty. But you are understand, they are angry.'

He turns back to the door and speaks to the young man, one of those who set on Jack earlier.

'¡Tú! ¡Pídale disculpas a su señoría escocés!'

The youth scowls, and shambles grudgingly to the doorway. 'Lo siento, señor ... Voy ahora. I go,' he says, and disappears into the school.

'I suppose that will do,' Jack says, in his haughty voice. 'And I hope they remember that Scotland is not England!' He pauses, and lets curiosity get the better of him. 'But you said they were angry? Why so? Why were they angry?'

The man – who introduces himself as the deputy master – is only too willing to tell Jack the news. Just that morning, word has come that 'Rey Carlos de Inglaterra' has declared war on Spain. And not only that. England has entered a pact with the Dutch, who just sixteen years before had won their independence from Spanish rule.

'Los estudiantes, the students, they hear una expedición come, perhaps to here like before with Drake, and then to Cadiz, to take our fleet of tresoro ... um, oro y plata, gold, silver, de las américas. We are know now you are Scotland, but then we not know. So los estudiantes, they mistake you for un chico ingles who we refused. He is here dos, tres weeks before. It is suspicion now because he is come from los hugonotes. The leader of the English expedición, el duque de Buck'ham, he is support the hogonotes also. So you see ...' the man shrugs, turning his palms up, as if this explains everything – which it does, near enough.

'By God! So England is at war with Spain?' Jack begins again to pace across the small room and back, realising that this means disaster for Robin and his plans.

I must ask Lorenzo to send a message to Conn. Or perhaps I can ride there and back tomorrow if I can borrow a horse. We must stop Robin. We must send him and Jeanne home. God only knows what will happen if Robin comes back here, blithely trying to join a crew to go to Cadiz! Ach, and what about his friend Miguel?

Keeping his frantic thoughts to himself, he faces the man.

'Gracias, señor. But now I must go. It is late and I have things to do.'

'Por supuesto mi señor ... Of course, my Lord Balfour. I am sorry the boys are a little rough.' He shrugs again, then points to the contents of Jack's pack, strewn on the floor. 'I help with your things.'

He begins to put everything back as Jack moves to the doorway.

'Lorenzo, Juanita, am I glad to see you!' He claps Lorenzo on the shoulder and gives Juanita a kiss, making her blush and giggle.

'I am here before,' she says. 'You are sit with book. I am come to speak, but the boys get you, put you in here. There is much talk, you are English spy, giving secret to hugonotes, to English king … I am fear for you. So I go tell Lorenzo and Bella at el Valentin.'

'Good God. Well, thank you so much for coming to find me, speaking to the maestro. I didn't know what was going on. But we're – I mean England's – at war! I must get a message to R … to my other friend, you know?' He stops himself saying Robin's name just in time, seeing the anxious expressions on his rescuers' faces. 'D'you think …' he begins, starting to walk away.

'You are forget your bag,' Lorenzo reminds him.

'Ach, thanks.' Jack turns back to the gatehouse. The deputy has put all Jack's things back in the pack, except for one item. It's in his hand, and his face is purple with rage.

'¡No un espía, sino un hereje!' he fumes. 'Not spy, heretic, no creyente – unbeliever!'

'What?' Jack, barely paying attention, reaches out, picks up his pack from the floor, swings it onto his shoulder, holds out his hand for the book.

'My book?'

'Tu libro? Your book? You are say it is yours?'

'Um …'

Lorenzo shoulders his way past Juanita and the deputy to stand by Jack.

'¿Hay algún problema, subdirector? ¡Mi señor Balfour tiene cosas que hacer! Debes dejarlo ir conmigo ahora.'

As he speaks, Lorenzo surreptitiously nudges Jack towards the door, where Juanita, looking pale, has her hands clasped over her mouth, her eyes wide in horror. Jack takes the hint, edging away, as Lorenzo and the deputy embark on what becomes a lengthy argument.

'Juanita,' he whispers to the girl, 'what are they saying? What's the matter now? Something about my book?'

'Ssh ... come quick, quiet. We go now.'

If Lorenzo is aware of what's happening outside, he gives no indication, although by going right into the room and facing the door himself, he ensures the Deputy Master keeps his back to it. Stealthily, Jack and Juanita creep at first a few feet, then a few yards, then, grabbing each others' hands, they run and run, into the safe darkness of the labyrinthine alleys.

Juanita is ahead, twisting and turning along the narrow alleys, staying in the shadows, her feet almost silent on the rough cobbles. Jack can only just keep up with her, not knowing the way she's taking, or even where she's leading him. His pack, slung over one shoulder, bangs hard against his back with every stride, but he barely notices.

Where is she taking me? Dear God, what next!

At last, Juanita dodges in through a wooden gate, slamming and bolting it shut as soon as Jack is through. As far as he can tell in the dark, they're in a small courtyard, hung with lines of laundry. Taking his hand again, the girl leads him, ducking under the sheets, the shirts, the shifts, and into a stable. Jack follows her as she weaves past the piles of hay, the rack of grooming gear, a couple of benches, and the horses, whickering in their stalls, startled by this disturbance.

'Come! Up!'

Juanita is climbing a ladder into a loft, strewn with straw. She flings herself down on the wooden boards, panting to get her breath back. Jack doubles over, hands on his knees, not so much out of breath as shocked by the sudden need to escape, confused as to why it was necessary, and full of admiration for Juanita, her quick thinking, and how fast she can run. He squats on the floor beside her, seeing her properly for the first time.

'Juanita, thank you, gracias. It seems you have saved me ... but I don't understand what from.'

'Oh Jack, it is el libro, the book! It is writ by el hereje, heretic Galileo. He say earth go round sun. Is loco, absurd! He was examine by la Inquisición of el Papa.'

Juanita grabs his hand, so appalled by the implication of his possessing such a book that she reverts to her own language.

'Es muy, muy peligroso tener este libro, especialmente aquí y ahora ... Very very danger have book here, now!'

'Really? Good God, I never thought ... Rab gave it to me ...'

'If we not run, la escuela, the marinero school, they take you to al sacerdote, the priest, and the priest, he must give you to los Inquisidores, and they ... oh Dios mío!'

'What? The Inquisition? They would hand me over to the Inquisition, and all because of a book? Good God, I didn't expect that!'

'But of course! Anyone who is not un verdadero católico, a true Catholic, is un hereje, heretic, this is how they say. Jack, truly, you do not want them to find you.'

Juanita pauses, not sure how much to tell this innocent young man about the danger he is skirting. She has grown up knowing the dangers of the tortures applied to suspects, the terrible outcomes of the trials against anyone regarded as not conforming absolutely to church doctrine, the auto-da-fé ritual that condemned heretics and apostates were put through. Supposedly a ceremony of public penitence, what it amounted to was public punishment, the victims being paraded through the towns, and then their sentences read out loud. Some – the lucky few – would be released. Some might escape with a whipping. Some were tortured again. And some, many, were finally burnt alive.

No, Juanita decides, *Jack no necesita saber todo esto. Not need to know all this.* She looks up at him.

'You know you cannot be seen here now, in streets? Is very danger. An-other time, per'aps you not get away!'

'But I must get the ship, the Orosia, the day after tomorrow! See, I have my passage booked!' He pulls the receipt from his boot and shows it to the girl, before stuffing it away again. 'How else can I get home?'

'No, you cannot. Please, you cannot go on Orosia. Es imposible. Los chicos de la escuela, they will be watch el puerto, the port, for you. They suspect you are un espía hugonote, but they wrong, so they very anger. But now they know you heretic. Will be recompensa if hand you in … and before then, I am fear they hurt you bad! Oh, but Jack, I am wonder, where is Robin? Is danger for him now also. My brother is expect go with him la próxima semana … um, week next?'

For a moment Jack is baffled, but Juanita explains that her brother is Miguel, who has become friends with Robin.

'Miguel, he say he and Robin go to Cadiz, then away, Americas. Pero ahora no es posible – now, for Miguel, yes per'aps he go, but Robin, is not possible.'

'Robin's gone to Santiago with his fiancée, Jeanne. They set off from Carral this morning – goodness, was it only this morning! I rode here with Conn and he spoke to Lorenzo, because his son Lucas has a ship they could take to Cadiz … Oh, Juanita, will Lorenzo be all right? We ran off and left him with that man!'

Juanita is not worried for Lorenzo.

'Lorenzo is big man here, If not, they would not let you go on his saying. He is importante, bien pensado. He belong cofradía … I not know word – men together, merchant, trade, artesano, posaderos.' She shrugs, unconcerned for her well-connected employer. 'El estara bien – he be good, no trouble. And I am work for him and Bella, so el me protegerá … he is protect me. But Miguel, I tell him now is not possible to go boat with Robin.'

She scrambles to her feet, brushing straw from her skirt, and seems about to descend the ladder.

'Wait! Where are you going? Should I come with you?' Jack asks, grabbing her arm and clutching her to him.

Juanita laughs and boldly gives him a brief kiss as she extracts her arm from his hold.

'No, stay here. Miguel is down. This is nuestra casa, our home, and this our establo, for horses. I fetch him.'

'But …'

Too late. She's gone.

CHAPTER EIGHTEEN

In Carral, Sara and Conn have just seen off their latest group of guests, a few bound for Santiago, the rest for A Coruña and their passage home. They're glad to see them go. They were quite a crowd, two groups of them, and all very excitable and talkative and loud. It's still early. The sun is barely warming the air, and the dew is fresh on the grass on either side of the lane, and sparkling from spiders' webs in the hedgerows. A blackbird is turning over last autumn's leaves, looking for his breakfast, and somewhere a wren is singing its heart out. Sara is looking forward to several quiet hours in her still room, concocting her lotions and potions, her simples and salves, while Conn has a mind to spend the day fishing. There's a large brown trout that's been eluding him in the Río da Brexa, less than ten minutes' walk away, and while the clouds are still lingering it's worth another try – and it'll be nice to sit for a while in the shade of the trees along the riverbank, gazing into the floes and eddies of the water. As they turn, arm in arm, to go back into el Hogar, their minds on their plans for the day, they're startled by the sound of hooves, and the sight of a pair of horses, rather wildly careering towards them from the direction of the village.

'They're in a hurry! I wonder what the matter is?'

As they stand by the door, puzzling, the riders come to a halt. One of them, bunching up her skirts, hurls herself off the saddle, as the other grasps the reins of her mount. With a shout – '¡Hasta luego!' – he and both horses are gone in a cloud of dust. The woman turns towards them.

'Conn, Sara, it's me!' She speaks with a deep Scottish accent and pulls her bonnet off her unruly mop of hair.

What the …? Who?

'It's me, Jack!'

'Jacobo? ¡Dios mío! ¿Lo que ha sucedido? Your face, se ve diferente!'

'Good God, Jack, you've shaved off your beard! And what on earth's happened since I left you yesterday? I think you'd better come inside.'

In the kitchen, ripping off the well-worn gown that covered his breeches and tunic, and downing a flagon of small beer, Jack gets his breath back.

'Oof, that's better. I'm so sorry to come charging in on you like this, but there's been some trouble, and ...'

'Slow down, lad – and sit down,' Conn says. 'Whatever it is, we'll sort it out. You're safe enough here. Now tell us what's happened.'

As quickly and as briefly as possible, Jack tells them. Sara's face turns pale with shock – and with the memories of her own flight from Léon, when all the Moriscos like herself, Catholic but of Muslim heritage, were expelled. Conn is outwardly calm, while his efficient mind is busily working out what now needs to be done.

'So Jack, you're wanted for being a heretic and Robin's wanted for being a Huguenot spy? God's teeth!' He gives a half-laugh. 'You couldn't make it up in a story, could you!'

'The thing is, I booked my passage for tomorrow, but ...'

'But it's not safe for you to be in A Coruña. Yes, I see that. So how did you get away?'

'You know Juanita, the maid who works for Lorenzo and Bella at el Valentin? She and her family helped me. They're so kind. Her mother insisted on giving me that dreadful bonnet and the old gown as a disguise, and her brother Miguel, Robin's new friend – well, that was him on the other horse. He's riding on to Santiago, to fetch Robin and Jeanne back here ...' Jack hesitates, suddenly unsure.

'Is that all right? I mean, for us to come here, Robin and me, being, well, on the run I suppose?'

Sara grasps his hand and gives it a squeeze. 'Por supuesto! We are family. Where else would you be going?'

'Of course,' Conn reassures him. 'So Miguel's gone to fetch Robin and Jeanne back, yes? They should still be on the road, somewhere between Ordes and A Igrexa I'd reckon, so it'll be easier for Miguel to find them than if they'd already got to Santiago. The horses will need a rest, but with luck, they should be back here tonight. Then what next, Jack? Any ideas?'

'Well, as I said, I was booked to go as a passenger on the Orosia tomorrow, but I can't now. So I'm afraid I've wasted a good half of the money you gave me,' Jack confesses sadly. 'But I still need to get home. And Robin does too. I just don't know how we can do it. Oh, and did you hear, King Charles has declared war on Spain!'

Once Conn and Sara have recovered from their astonishment at Jack's latest piece of news, the three of them begin to hatch a plan.

'As I see it,' Conn says, 'the sooner you're out of Spain the better, you and Robin. And I think you've two choices. You can either go overland, like you and Jeanne came, walking or riding mebbe, or you can go by sea. And ...'

'But neither Robin nor I can go back to A Coruña,' Jack interrupts. 'Even if Lorenzo managed to quash any further action being taken by the school, it's too risky, isn't it?'

'Aye, but that's not what I'm suggesting. There's another place, Betanzos. It's an estuary port, and beginning to rival A Coruña. I think ...'

This time it's Sara who interrupts.

'Yes, Betanzos, it is per'aps nueve millas, nine miles? Vera, you know, at the bakery, her son Vasco is fisherman there ... Oh!'

Sara suddenly realises the way Conn's mind is working. He grins at her.

'Exactly. If we could get these lads to Betanzos, I'm sure we could make it worth Vasco's while to take an extended trip past Ferrol and along the north coast ... and if they happened to get as far as Bayonne, just over the border into France, well, mebbe the lads could find a passage to Bordeaux, or even back to la Rochelle. How does that sound, Jack?'

Jack, anxious to get away while at the same time regretting the need to leave these kind people, thinks it sounds marvellous, but for one thing.

'It'll be quite a long trip, won't it?' he asks, frowning.

'Ah, yes, I'm afraid so. Vasco's only got a small fishing boat, and I imagine he'll need to do some fishing on the way. It'd be a bit suspicious otherwise, don't you think?' Conn replies. 'You're thinking of getting back to your work at the mill, and your ideas for your bakery, aren't you?'

Sarah gives her husband a puzzled look, knowing nothing about any of this, but Jack nods, smiling ruefully, as his hopes for the future splinter and crash around him like shards of glass …

'Aye, I am. I won't be back in time for MacMorran – I'd only just have made it, even if I'd been able to go on the Orosia. Without my work at the mill, well, there's no way I can fund what needs to be done at the Tor. So much for all my plans …' He pauses, looking glum. 'And young Robin won't be setting off to the Americas either. Goodness knows what wild idea he'll come up with next! Ach, I was so excited about going home, and now it's all gone wrong. My plans were all for nothing.'

Whisked away by Miguel, frustratingly within sight of the great cathedral of Santiago de Compostela, Robin and Jeanne are both quiet on the ride back to Carral, absorbing what they'd just been told: that Jack is in danger of being handed over to the Inquisition for possessing Rab's book by Galileo Galilei, and that Robin himself is wanted as a spy, supposedly working for the Huguenots and the English. None of it seems to make any sense, but that hardly matters. The fact is they need to leave as soon as possible.

'I not know how you go,' Miguel had told them, 'but Jack, he is with Conn and Sara. They think of way. Robin, you understand you cannot come to Cádiz. Is too peligrosso … perilous?

'Aye, I understand,' Robin agrees reluctantly. 'But what about you, Miguel? What will you do?'

'Ah, for me is not peligrosso until war arrive, and per'aps even not then. Our fleet is not strong, after the sea battle with your friends, the hugunotes,' Miguel replies, with a wry smile, 'but even so, the English, their fleet is not as it was in the olden days. So I go Cádiz. Even if war, barcos mercantes, merchant ship, it go los americas, and I go. I sorry you cannot come. Per'aps en otro momento, other time?'

'Ach, I wish!'

Once they reach el Hogar, and the relieved welcome of Jack, Sara, and Conn, Miguel only stays long enough to give his two tired horses a long drink, as he swiftly downs a tankard of ale and makes short work of the cold meat, cheese and bread that Sara insists they all share. Now he has gone, and Robin and Jeanne eagerly listen to the plan that Jack, Sara, and, principally, Conn, have worked out for how for the three youngsters might get away.

'First of all, we must get to a place called Betanzos,' Jack tells them, 'and after that it relies on a fisherman, Vera's son Vasco, being willing to take us to the border in his boat, the Peto Real.'

It's a damn shame I can't go with Miguel, Robin is thinking. I was so set on it. What an adventure it would have been, all that way across the Atlantic to the Americas! Ach, but I reckon being a wanted man, and escaping on some old fishing boat, well that's a bit of an adventure too!

'We need to allow a couple of hours to get to Vasco's house,' Conn adds. 'I've already had a word with Vera, while we were waiting for you two to get back, and she's sure he'll help ... She says he usually goes out with the morning tide, just himself and his son. So, I'd like to get away ...'

'You're coming too?'

'Aye, Robin, I am. I reckon I'd better make sure you all get safely out of the country, don't you? And I can crew for Vasco on the way back. Vera says his wife and boy will look after the horses while we're gone, and ...'

'Um ...'

Conn stops speaking, as Jeanne suddenly gets up from her chair, its feet making a terrible scraping noise on the hard floor.

Pale as ice, her lips compressed into a tight line, her hands are twisting together as if of their own accord.

'Jeanne? You are ill? Or …'

'No, Sara, I'm not ill, thank you. I'm sorry, Robin, so sorry, but I am not coming.'

'What?' Robin leaps to his feet, grabs her arm. 'What d'you mean, you're not coming? You heard what Conn said. We have to leave, and now, tonight!'

Sara, Conn, and Jack glance at each other, eyebrows raised, shrugging slightly and shaking their heads in surprise.

'Jeanne, Robin, per'aps we leave you a minute, to talk?' Sara is now also on her feet, gesturing to Conn and Jack to do the same.

'No!' Robin shouts, dropping Jeanne's arm again. 'Sorry, I didn't mean to shout. Sorry. But if Jeanne has something to say, she can say it to all of us.' He turns to face her. 'You never said anything, all the time we were coming back here with Miguel. You knew we had to leave, he'd told us so. I don't understand what …'

'Please,' Jeanne says, 'please all sit, please.'

As they do as she asks, Jeanne swallows, takes a deep breath, and begins to explain.

'Robin, you are right. I say nothing on the way here. It is too sudden, what Miguel tell us, that you and Jacques are not safe, that you are being wanted. I am feared. Now I am hear this plan of go in bateau de pêche, fisherman boat, back to France. And I am seeing,' she pauses, giving Robin what passes for a smile, 'that already you are think that this, c'est une autre excitation, another exciting adventure, non?'

'Well yes. It is exciting,' he admits, shrugging. 'Scary of course, but Jack and Conn and this fisherman will be there too …'

'Oui, so you will be safe, and that is good.' Jeanne smiles properly now, sitting down again next to Robin, taking his hand and looking directly into his blue eyes. 'You will go home to Surgères – and then what? I am think, Robin, that for you this is not enough. America, no, you cannot go, but I am think you not ready, how are you say, to settle? You are want more adventure, per'aps more in the ships, and this ...'

'Och, of course!' Robin breaks in. 'I truly think that's the life for me, being a mariner, a merchant seaman I hope, and ...'

'... and this, it is good, to have this ambition. I am seeing it is make you more alive, more 'appy, than you were on the farm or in the town, and with more purpose. There is much for you to do, to learn, les voyages vers de nouveaux endroits, many journeys, voyages, and new places. But Robin, think of how it is for me, yes? I am not want to sit with your maman while you are away, until you are ready to be marrying. I 'ave lived at Surgères all my life. I can do more, while you are doing ... well, whatever you are doing! So I think, per'aps ...' she falters, realising she's relying on Sara and Conn's agreement, looking across at them, with something close to desperation in her eyes. '... per'aps can I stay here, like you are invite me before, when Robin is go to Cádiz and the America?'

Jeanne is still looking anxiously at her hosts, but when Sara smiles, she is filled with relief.

'Of course!' Sara says. 'Of course, yes, you can stay here. It is as we said before. You will be help to me when Conn is away, and we will be like family together, yes? There, all is agreed. No es un drama. So, Jack and Conn, you go now to get the horses ready, and I will get food in bag for you. Oof, three men, I will need gran bolsa, very big bag!'

Smiling and uncharacteristically fussing, Sara ushers Conn and Jack away from the table, leaving Robin and Jeanne alone. They both stand, move towards the other, hesitate.

'Jeanne, are you sure?'

'Oh Robin, oui, yes, I am sure,' she replies, taking the last step towards him as he holds out his arms, snuggling gladly into his embrace. 'You are the man of my 'art, and we are promised. There is no-one else for me. But we are young still. There is not a rushing. When we are ready, I think I like to be marrying you,' she blushes, 'but it is for me as it is for you. I need to do some other thing first. I need to 'ave time, to be myself. Then, after, we will be together.'

CHAPTER NINETEEN

The departure of the three men from el Hogar is quick. There are loving hugs and kisses, promises to stay safe, not to take risks, for Robin and Jack to send word when they've arrived in Surgères, and, in Conn's case, to come home soon. The bag of provisions is fastened with the other packs onto Conn's horse, Canela, and, with one last kiss for Sara, he sets a steady pace, leading the way north through the half-dark. Jack and Robin are sharing a saddle on Conn's long-suffering cob, Mazorca.

'Are you all right, mate?' Robin asks his friend about an hour after they've left Carral. 'You've been awful quiet.'

'Ach, Robin, I'm sorry. It's just, well, I suppose I'm coming to terms with things, you know, how everything's changed.'

'Isn't that what you wanted? To make a total break from routine? I know I did!'

'Aye, you're right, I did – and by God I have! But I'm not sure what I'll be going back to. I'm pretty sure I'll have lost my place at the mill and the bakery … and if I'm honest, Robin, I don't think I want to go back to living at Hawkhill. Aunt Elspeth and Uncle Will are the kindest and best people – but …'

'But you've grown out of them, your family? Aye, I feel the same. I can't see myself back at Marans or Surgères.'

The two young men fall silent for a while. The only sounds are the horses' hooves, the occasional shriek as an owl swoops and catches his supper, and the eerie and haunting songs of the nightbirds. The air is still, the stars bright in a clear but moonless night. When Jack suddenly laughs, it takes Robin so much by surprise that he almost falls off.

'Oops! You nearly lost me there! What is it, Jack? What are you laughing at?'

'Myself!' Jack guffaws. 'Here I am, doing a moonlight flit from the Inquisition with two good mates, and a bonnie lassie back at home ... and I've been fretting myself into a real misery. Well, enough of that! Let's assume that we make it safely back to your parents. Then what? You say you can't see yourself back with them, so what can you see for yourself, eh? Are you serious about becoming a mariner? It's not just a fantsy?'

'Ach, no, Jack, I truly am serious. I really do see myself on the merchant ships, learning, like I said, working my way up, until one day I have one of my own. I know that'll be a big responsibility, but I think it'd be marvellous. It's what I want. That's what going to the Americas would have been about,' Robin replies, somewhat plaintively, his mind returning to the hopes that were so nearly realised, and so recently dashed.

'Aye, but could you nae do it just as well somewhere else? I mean, somewhere other than Spain?'

'Well yes, in theory. Spain's out of the question now, but Bordeaux and La Rochelle will be just as dangerous – you know, because of the Huguenots? The middle of a war zone isn't ideal for any kind of shipping, let alone merchants!'

Jack laughs again. 'Aye, but Robin, I'm thinking, could you not do it out of Leith mebbe? There are ships going all over, and ...'

'Well yes, of course. Leith would be damn nigh perfect ...' he pauses, shakes his head resignedly. 'But I grew up in Fife, and we left there years ago. I don't know anyone there anymore, let alone in Leith.'

'Mebbe not, but I do! Not just Master Flint and Sam and Daan on the Eagle, but quite a few others that I used to have a drink and a blether with when I was fetching the grain for the mill.'

'Och, Jack, d'you mean ... could you introduce me to them, perhaps recommend me? Is that what you're meaning? Jack, that'd be great!'

'I can't promise anything, mind,' Jack says hastily, 'but I'm willing to try. At the very least you'd get a place on a crew, start at the bottom again. It'd be something definite to tell your parents when we get back to them, eh? We could go on to Scotland together, and mebbe you could stay with Will and Elspeth? It'd be different for you – they're not family! And you'd be away a lot ...'

'But would they have room for me, along with Davie and Harry and you?'

'Ach nae, I wouldna' be there, so there'd be room enough.'

'Oh! So whe ...'

Robin never has the chance to complete his question. Conn has pulled Canela to a halt. Mazorca and the boys come alongside.

'We'll be getting into Betanzos in a few minutes, lads,' Conn says, unusually sternly. 'I know it's the middle of the night, but best not to talk, eh? I doubt word will have got this far about you two renegades, but I don't want to take any risks. So if anyone stops us, or speaks to us, let me do the talking.'

'Oh, right. Not a word.'

Slightly shaken by this timely reminder that their ride through the night isn't for pleasure, the two younger men fall silent. They follow Conn and Canela through the vast Arco da Pont Nova gateway in the town walls, along the steeply sloping narrow streets, past the clock tower, the two churches dedicated to Saint Francis and Saint James, the marketplace, and the taverns, and on to the riverside. As Conn had hoped, the fishermen are already busily preparing to sail out with the morning tide.

Phew! We made it in time! Jack thinks, elbowing Robin in the ribs and grinning.

Conn has already dismounted, handing Canela's reins to Jack.

'Wait here,' he whispers, 'and stay quiet.'

They watch as he confidently strides across to the cluster of men, busily loading nets and crates.

'¡Hola! Busco a Vasco ... Ah, ahí estás,' they hear him call, as one of the fishermen comes to meet him. Conn is speaking more quietly now, as he and Vasco come back to where they wait with the horses. They see Vasco nod, and Conn passes him a small bag. Weather-beaten and wiry, Vasco eyes them for a long moment. Finally, just as they fear he's about to turn them away, he smiles.

'¿Entonces eres mi tripulación para mi largo viaje? New crew for long voyage? Bienvenidos, wel-come! Mi hijo Simeón se llevará sus caballos a casa. Ven, debemos irnos rápido.'

A lad of about twelve has joined them.

'Papá, ¿qué está pasando?'

As Simeón and his father have a hasty conversation, and the small bag is passed over, Conn explains to Jack and Robin.

'Vasco is pleased to take us as his new crew,' he says with a wink. 'We're only just in time. His son here will take the horses home and explain to Vasco's wife.'

Conn pulls a face, not envying the boy that task, but there's no time to do anything else, and he hopes that perhaps the bag of coins he's given Vasco will mollify her. The next few minutes vanish in a flurry of activity. Conn, Robin, and Jack grab their various bags and packs from Canela, Conn gives the reins to Simeón –

'Gracias!'

'Es bueno. ¡Prefiero los caballos a pescar!'

– and they follow Vasco on board.

'Sit now, work after,' Vasco says tersely, as he concentrates on steering the small craft through the maze of sandbanks that are gradually appearing as the tide flows out. On either side of the river, the few buildings are soon left behind, the green vegetation disappears, and the earliest of the sea birds dives down to take its breakfast from the shoals of tiny fish. The breeze is fresh, the air increasingly salty. Jack sighs with pleasure and turns to his companions with a smile.

'Homeward bound, eh? Now Robin, what was it you were going to ask me?'

THE END

AUTHOR'S NOTE

I am proud of the fact that Johne (**Jack**) Balfour, was my 8th great grandfather.

However, 'Course Adjustments' is a work of fiction, loosely woven around historical fact.

Any factual and chronological alterations and errors, deliberate or otherwise, are my own.

ACKNOWLEDGEMENTS

I am grateful to Wendy, Bea, Linda, Bonny, Abbey, Rosemary and Shirley who endured and encouraged throughout all the adjustments to this story.

I also owe to debt of gratitude to Elizabeth, RPS, and the whole team at novum publishing for their faith in my writing: thank you!

Johne (**Jack**) Balfour married Jennet/Janet **(Jennie)** Tullois. They settled in St. Andrews, where their four children were born. Their first child, John, was born in 1628 and died aged 3 in 1631, the same year that their second son, also named John, was born. He was my 7th great grandfather. Jack and Jennie's daughters Elspeth and Christen were born in 1634 and 1639 respectively.

I have not yet found any further information about Jack's brothers Alexander (**Sandy**) or Hendrie (**Harry**) Balfour. Their brother David (**Davie)** married Margarett Gairdner in Kirkcaldy, Fife, and they subsequently had two children, Mitchall and Allison.

William (**Will**) Balfour, my 9th great granduncle, and Elisabeth (**Elspeth**), my 9th great grandaunt, are both elusive. Will seems to have become confused, in various publications and family trees, with his second cousin, General Sir William Balfour (d.1660).

Robert **(Rab)** Logan died in Edinburgh in 1651, his wife **Jesette** (aka Janet) Cosse died in 1658. Their son Robert (**Robin**) Logan married **Jeanne Rouen** (aka Jean Rowan) in 1631. I have not found any further definite information about them, nor about Robin's brother John (**Jon**).

Benjamin de Rohan, Duc de Soubise was defeated in September 1625 and lost control of the Île de Ré. A third Huguenot rebellion (backed by the British king, Charles I, as part of the Anglo-French War) ended with the surrender of La Rochelle in 1628. The elder brother of Soubise, Henri de Rohan, continued to resist the French crown in southern France, but was finally defeated in June 1629. The Huguenots lost their land and rights and were actively persecuted by Louis XIV. Soubise fled to England, where he died in 1642. His body was buried in Westminster Abbey.

The ***Escuela de Muchachos del Mar*** (School of the Boys of the Sea) at A Coruña was later joined to the Hospital of San Andrés.

Santiago de Compostela remains a popular destination for pilgrims and other walkers. Ferrol and A Coruña are the traditional starting points within Spain for the Camino Ingles, the route taken by seafaring pilgrims from northern Europe, and which links up with the Celtic Caminos in the UK and Ireland. This lesser-known route passes alongside the Ria de Betanzos, with views of the tidal estuary and the surrounding marshlands.

The port of **Leith** is today Scotland's largest enclosed deep-water port. It has twenty working berths and is capable of handling ships up to 50,000 DWT and in excess of 1M tonnes of cargo. It has two dry docks, and the Ocean Terminal is the permanent berth for the now-retired royal yacht Britannia.

The author

A perennial bookworm and student, Maggie Williams Richmond has enjoyed a varied career including nursing, social care management, and charity administration. Having formerly balanced work and travel, Maggie spent the first five years of her retirement labouring with her husband to restore an old stone house in the foothills of the French Pyrenees. At the same time, she continued to compose songs, write poems, and publish a quirky reflective blog, co-authored with her dog Shadow. Now settled near Dundee, Maggie has delved deeply into her family tree and is developing a series of stories based on the lives of her ancestors – a very mixed bunch, including a much-maligned Scottish nobleman, a transported convict, a Welsh preacher, and a Belfast industrialist. When not writing, researching, cooking, or gardening, you may find Maggie tricycling into town, walking along the coast path, or helping out at the local PDSA charity shop.

Maggie Williams Richmond

Costly Truths

ISBN 978-3-99131-376-2
154 pages

Set against the backdrop of King James' accession to the English throne, this debut novel combines historical accuracy and authentic Scots idiom in a tale of love, death, and betrayal, as a young woman discovers the depths of her husband's duplicity.